Second Chances

Samantha Baca

Just One Time

Second Chances

Third Time's The Charm

Four-ever Single

Fifth Wheel

Cover Design: Richard Baca
Image(s): DepositPhotos

Contents

Contents

<u>One</u>
Jane

"Alright, who's next?" I asked, looking at the charts spread out on the raised ledge of the nurse's station. Usually, they were lined up and organized, however, we had a temp filling in for us this week, so nothing was where I expected it.

"You've got Frank Townsend waiting for you in room one—but be warned, he's a bit of a hothead this morning. Then Olivia Rosario is here for her one-year wellness check. She's in room two." Sabrina, one of the nurse techs, smiled as she brushed past me, grabbing the charts and handing me the one I needed. She'd been with our practice the longest, and I loved everything about her.

"Thank you," I said while glancing over the paper attached to the clipboard. "Why am I seeing Frank?"

"He wants to discuss options for Hattie. She just turned fifteen." Sabrina raised her eyebrows and scrunched her face.

"Gotcha."

It wasn't unusual to discuss birth control options with parents on occasion, but I wasn't quite in the mindset to deal with Frank this morning. He was the town grump, a single father, and most likely here to yell and complain about how his little girl wasn't so little anymore.

"Is there more coffee?" I asked, looking helplessly at her.

"I'll have Tina start a new pot," she laughed, her eyes traveling over to the temp sitting at the computer, staring as if it was going to tell her what to do. "But on the bright side, as soon as you're done with Frank, you get some nice eye candy in room 2."

I felt my cheeks flush as she wiggled her eyebrows suggestively.

Dominic was new in town and had only been in Beaumont Creek for a month, if that. His parents, however, have lived here for over twenty years, and everyone in town simply adored them. When he showed up unexpectedly and bought the house next door, everyone noticed. But it was the beautiful baby girl he brought with him that had won over most of the women.

"I'm here to help kids, not hit on their fathers," I hissed out, tapping her shoulder with the chart as I passed her on my way to room one.

"Why not multitask?" she teased, tossing a wink over her shoulder as she popped into another room to collect vitals while I headed off to deal with Frank.

I opened the door and pulled my shoulders back, preparing myself the best I could.

"Good morning, Frank," I said, offering my hand, which he barely took before pulling away and pacing across the small room.

I held the chart against my chest, wondering what the best way was to approach him.

"What can I do for you?"

There, just get straight to the point.

"I need to talk to you about Hattie."

"Okay. What's going on?"

"Well, as you may know, she just turned fifteen."

I nodded.

"Well, it probably comes as no surprise that some of the boys at school are taking *an interest* in her."

"Okay," I said slowly. "What is it that you'd like my help with?"

I assumed he was getting to the point of asking about getting a pamphlet he could use to talk to her about the birds and the bees or maybe to request to bring her in so I could speak with her.

"I need you to tell her not to have sex. I've already told her it's forbidden, but I would appreciate her hearing it from a medical professional."

I pulled my head back, my eyes feeling as if they were about to pop out of my head.

"I'm sorry, what?"

"I need you to tell her that she cannot have sex. Scare the temptation out of her by giving her horror stories if you have to—just make sure she gets the point loud and clear."

His voice boomed so loud that I was surprised the framed pictures on the wall didn't come tumbling down.

I set the chart down and folded my arms over my chest as I stared at him.

"Frank, I will not do that. And honestly—you shouldn't either. Sex is a normal—"

"Like hell it is!"

"Lower your voice," I warned sternly. "There are children in the other rooms, and I will not have you in here yelling and causing a scene."

"Then do your damn job!"

I pulled in a deep breath and slowly forced it through my lips while I tried to regain my composure.

"My job is to care for children, not to lie to them. If you'd like to bring Hattie in to see me, I'd be more than happy to sit down and talk to her about her body, the changes it's going through, making smart choices, and contraception options for when she's ready."

"Like hell you will!"

His face turned red as he clenched his fists at his sides.

"Then it seems we're done here, Frank. You need to leave."

"You're not going to help me?" he bellowed.

"You're not asking for help. You're asking me to lie to your daughter because you're too afraid to tell her the truth. Hattie is a smart girl, Frank, and you've raised her well. If you give her the knowledge and resources to make good decisions, she will. But if you hide stuff from her and keep her from learning how to protect herself, she's going to find herself in a position she doesn't want to be in."

He pushed a hand through his hair, sighing heavily as his stained t-shirt lifted on his stomach.

"What's that supposed to mean?"

"It means that kids are going to do what they want, no matter how hard you try to stop them. If Hattie wants to have sex, she's going to. If she doesn't want to have sex, then she needs to know that she's in control of her body and how to voice her choices. Forbidding sex doesn't give her that message. You're only hurting her by not allowing her access to the information she needs to make good decisions. If she doesn't know how to protect herself, she could end up pregnant or with an STD. Those aren't things you want for her, yet you're unwilling to give her the tools she needs."

"I'll be the one to decide what she needs." He grabbed his ball cap from the exam table, shoved it on his head, and then stormed out of the room, slamming the door behind him.

I shook my head, trying to clear it so I could move on to the next patient.

When I came out of the room, I found a handful of techs lingering nearby, whispering as they looked my way.

"Everything is fine," I assured them, holding my hand up as Nick approached. He was the only male nurse on our staff, but he was damn good at his job, and all single mothers simply adored him. It was probably because he was as good-looking as he was charming. But given that he was fifteen years younger than me and worked for me, he was officially off limits. Even if my sister and Nate constantly tried to set us up shortly after Nick started renting Nate's house.

"Can you please make a note to follow up with Frank in two weeks? I'd like to revisit our discussion and see if he'd be interested in having a conversation with Hattie together."

Sabrina nodded as she slid into the chair behind the desk and started typing.

I set the chart down on the counter and grabbed the one for room two. My stomach fluttered nervously, and I had to remind myself that it was just from the interaction with Frank, not because I was excited to see Dominic. He was just here for his daughter's well-check. That was it.

My fingers trembled slightly as I knocked on the door before pushing it open.

He was standing at the exam table, holding her up as she held onto his fingers, bouncing excitedly as her little giggles filled the room. Dark eyes locked onto mine as I admired the way his short hair looked so soft with the fade on the side and how his t-shirt pulled tightly around his biceps.

"Good morning, Doctor Hughes," he greeted, the dimples in his cheeks winking at me.

He grabbed Olivia and held her to his chest as I closed the door behind me.

"Good morning," I replied with a genuine smile, my voice flirtier than I would have liked. "How's Miss Olivia doing? Is she feeling better?"

Dominic had brought her in two weeks ago for a cold, which seemed to resolve quickly, given how energetic and bubbly she was.

She reached for me, so I held my hands out and took her, letting her play with the stethoscope wrapped around my neck.

"She's doing a lot better, thank you. I appreciate you getting us in on such short notice."

"It was no problem at all," I assured him, feeling those pesky butterflies in my stomach again when I looked at him.

"I'm happy to hear that she's doing well," I continued, trying to focus on the adorable, squirmy patient in my arms and not her attractive father. "Let's get started with our exam, shall we?" I smacked my lips together a few times, making loud popping noises that had her giggling all over again. I smiled brightly as I set her on the exam table and leaned against it, keeping her secure.

"Overall, how are things going for you guys?" I asked, looking up at him while moving the stethoscope over her back and listening to her lungs.

"Pretty good." He nodded, his arms folded over his chest, making it look even more impressive.

"How's her eating? Is she still interested in trying new foods?"

He shook his head and scrunched his face.

"She'll try new things here and there but prefers to stick with her favorites."

"So, a lot of French toast sticks and carrots?" I glanced up to find a cheesy grin spread across her face. I remembered him mentioning them to me when he was worried about her lack of appetite with her cold and how she was refusing them.

"That girl loves her carrots."

I tapped her little nose with my finger and then continued with the exam.

"That's a great thing," I assured him. "Kids who enjoy fruits and vegetables at this age continue eating them with little pushback. Definitely keep offering them to her. Just make sure they're cut into appropriate sizes, so she doesn't choke."

"Will do."

I laid her down on the table and tickled her little feet before pressing on her tummy. She was by far one of the happiest, easiest infants I'd worked with in a while, and I felt myself have a sudden rush of baby fever.

I lifted her off of the table and handed her back to her father while I jotted down some notes in her chart.

"Everything looks great; she's right on track for where she needs to be," I said, sitting down on the stool and smiling as he sat on the bench and held her. "Do you have any questions for me today?"

"Actually, I do," he said, somewhat nervously. "As you know, I'm new to town and haven't really had the time to get to know anyone. While my parents take care of Olivia during the day while I'm at work, I'd like to start getting involved in some play dates or get-togethers on the weekends. Maybe socialize her with other kids and meet other single parents. Do you think it's too early for that?"

"Not at all. I think it's a wonderful idea. It's never too early to introduce her to other kids her age."

"Do you, by chance, know of any *single* parents that might be up for hanging out?"

Something about the way he asked it shot nerves straight through my stomach again. *Was he flirting with me?*

I sighed heavily, forcing myself to remember to breathe.

"Umm, not offhand, but then again, I don't really get out and socialize much these days, either." I laughed awkwardly.

"So you're a single parent, too?"

I nodded.

"My kids are nine and seven. Mikey and Sally."

His brows pulled together for a moment while he bounced Olivia on his knee.

"Wait a minute—are you Mikey's mom? Mikey Hughes?"

Now it was my turn to eye him suspiciously.

"Yeah, why?"

"I'm his new teacher—Mr. Rosario. I just took over for Mrs. Crawford; she started her maternity leave this week."

My eyes nearly bulged out of my head.

"Oh! I'm so sorry. I hadn't even put the two together until now. Of course, that makes sense. I have it on my calendar for the parent-teacher conference next week, but I totally forgot that she was heading out on leave soon."

"Well, I guess I'll see you next week."

My mind was still spinning for a moment while I processed that not only had I been entertaining dirty thoughts about the father of one of my patients, but I was also now having them about my son's new teacher. As if that couldn't get any more complicated.

"Yes. I will see you then."

My throat was suddenly dry, the words struggling to make their way out.

He stood up, grabbed the diaper bag from the bench beside him, and lifted Olivia to his hip.

"See you around, Doctor Hughes." He stopped briefly, resting his hand on the doorknob before turning it. "Oh, and if you're interested in a play date, just let me know."

<u>Two</u>
Jane

"It *IS* that big of a deal," I whined, taking a sip of wine as Abby bustled around the kitchen, looking for the rosemary.

"Why? Just because he's going to be Mikey's teacher?" She looked at me over her shoulder before smiling at Penny sitting in the highchair next to me, then turned back to the food she had cooking on the stove.

"Not just that, but he's also the father of one of my patients," I stressed.

"Who just turned one and has no idea what's going on?"

"He's just a baby," I continued. "He's younger than me, Abby. Like *a lot* younger than me. He's barely thirty-two—I'm *TEN* years older! Who would even want to date an old bag like me?"

"Oh please, you're not old," she scolded as she shook the spices into the skillet and then stirred it.

"I'm not young. I can't do all the things guys his age expect women to do." I lifted the glass to my lips and took another drink as Penny sat there, judging me.

"What exactly do you think he expects you to do?" She set the spatula on the counter and turned to face me. "And how do you know how old he is? Did you ask him?"

My face turned beet red as I took another sip. I couldn't tell if it was the wine that was making my cheeks flush or the embarrassment of going through his daughter's chart to find information on him.

"Jane?" she questioned, eyebrow raised. "Tell me you did not go through his personal information on file at your work."

"We needed to make sure we had everything updated in Olivia's file," I shrugged. "I *might have* come across a form that had his date of birth listed on it."

She shook her head and tsked at me.

"Jane, Jane, Jane," she sighed.

"What's going on?" Nate asked, coming into the kitchen with a goofy grin on his face when he spotted his baby girl. "Hey my lucky Penny."

"Nothing," I lied, getting up and giving him my seat so he could be with his daughter.

"Oh, it's something alright," Abby teased.

"Spill it," Nate coaxed, looking between us. "Cause you know Abby is going to tell me as soon as you leave the room."

I arched an eyebrow at my little sister, pretending that this was some sort of shocking news.

Then I rolled my eyes and laughed.

"Abby's the worst at keeping secrets."

"So then you should just tell me yourself," Nate said, popping a grape into his mouth from the platter sitting on the island in front of him.

"It's nothing, really."

"She has a crush," Abby rushed out, her eyes widening with delight as she watched me blush.

"Is this something going on between you and Capshaw again?" Nate asked, looking from his wife to me. "Because I gotta admit, he's been in a good mood lately, which usually only means one thing."

"No," I laughed. "That was one time, Nate. One. Time."

Okay, so it was technically more than one time. We had been secretly messing around for a few weeks before we got caught. From then on, I'd only ever admitted to it happening once.

"And he never got over it," he teased. "Walking around like a wounded puppy, his heart torn to shreds—"

"You just said he was in a good mood lately," I interrupted, calling him on his shit.

He shrugged, smirked, and pushed another grape into his mouth.

"So, who's the guy?"

"No one," I rushed out, giving Abby *the look* before she could say anything more. I heard voices coming down the hallway as Mikey and Sally headed toward the kitchen with my parents right behind them.

The last thing I wanted was for Mikey to hear that his mom had the hots for his new teacher. It was hard enough for kids in school to be teased by other kids for random stuff, but add in your mom doing your teacher, and that was a level of embarrassment that many didn't easily overcome. I wasn't going to do that to him.

"So," my mother said, effectively changing the subject. "Your father and I are going camping in two weeks, and since you'll be working and the kids will be on spring break, we wanted to see if we could take them with us."

I looked from them to the kids, noticing how excited they looked about it.

"Um, well, I'm not sure," I answered. "I'd have to talk to Rick. I don't know if he had any plans for Spring Break."

"Oh, please," my mom snorted. "When was the last time he took time off of work to do something with them during one of their breaks?"

I arched an eyebrow at her in a warning. While it was no secret that my ex-husband was a shitty father, I still tried to keep anyone from bashing him in front of the kids. At the end of the day, he was still their dad, and they deserved the opportunity to decide how they felt about him on their own.

"As I said, I'll discuss it with Rick."

It killed me that I couldn't take time off this year for their spring break, but it also made me feel somewhat relieved that my parents were interested in taking them for the entire week. They loved camping, so this would be a fun trip for them, as long as Rick didn't put up a fight.

I had full custody, but I still tried to make an effort to include him in their lives as often as I could. Not for me, but for them.

Everyone started talking about other stuff as they moved around the kitchen, getting ready to sit for dinner. But for me, my mind was still distracted by something I couldn't have.

Three
Dominic

"No, Ma, she doesn't need any more toys." I pressed the phone between my ear and neck while I stirred the macaroni and cheese in the pot on the stove. "I know it was her first birthday, but you guys already spoiled her with a ton of stuff on her actual birthday. We don't need to have a big party for her with people we don't even know. Dinner with you and dad was more than enough."

I could feel the frustration radiating through the phone as my mom fought to get her way. I knew it was only a matter of time before she hung up and came over instead. The joys of living next door to each other.

I stopped moving for a moment, trying to hear if she was still on the line. Just like clockwork, the doorbell rang. I chuckled as I set my phone down on the counter before rushing to open the door. I'd learned quickly to lock it if I didn't want her to just barge in. Sure, she had a spare key, but we'd come to the agreement that it was only to be used for emergencies. This was just part of the conditions of me moving to Beaumont Creek and living next to her.

"Hello, mother, what a lovely surprise," I joked sarcastically as she rolled her eyes and came inside, swatting at me as my father followed behind her.

"Well, I figured your *phone* was having problems again, since you couldn't seem to understand what I was saying. It left me no choice but to stop by and talk about this in person."

She brushed past me, straight to the pack-n-play where Olivia was busy playing with some blocks.

"She's fine in there, you know? Playing and exploring her world," I teased as she picked her up. My mother cuddled Olivia to her chest as if she hadn't just spent most of the day with her before I picked her up after work.

I arched an eyebrow at my father, who just shrugged his shoulders and plopped down on the couch. He was used to it as much as I was by now.

"She needs some grandma time, doesn't she," my mom cooed, bouncing Olivia as she giggled.

"You guys want to stay for dinner?" I asked, heading back to the stove and praying that the mac and cheese hadn't burned in the few minutes I'd been away. I'd turned the burner off but forgot to move the pan.

Thankfully, it looked fine and didn't smell burned. I'd come to expect that my parents would drop in occasionally, so I'd started making extra food as a standard. If they didn't come by, then it benefited me by having leftovers for lunch the next day. Win-win.

"No thanks, we're meeting some friends for dinner at Surf 'N Shack here in a bit," my mom answered, still not looking at me. "But I wanted to talk to you about Olivia's birthday. I know you don't want to have a big party for her, but I think it would do you some good to meet people around town, especially kids her age that she can start playing with."

"So you want me to go around and ask random strangers to come to my kid's party?" I asked with a bit too much sarcasm as I scooped some mac and cheese into a bowl for Olivia. "I'm pretty sure that's going to give me a reputation that I don't want around here."

"Don't be silly," my mom scoffed, sitting Olivia in her highchair. "But it wouldn't hurt you to find some friends who also have young kids."

My mind immediately traveled to Doctor Hughes, and I felt that same weird feeling rush over me the way it did when I was in her office. It was the strangest thing, but I felt so drawn to her that I found it hard to think about anything other than her this week. I wasn't one who usually looked forward to parent-teacher conferences, but I couldn't wait to see her again at Mikey's.

"It's this Saturday at one o'clock. Your father and I can pick you up if you want to go together, or we can—"

"What?" I had been so lost in my thoughts that I hadn't heard a word she'd said.

My mother sighed heavily, took the bowl of macaroni out of my hand, and sat down beside Olivia to feed her.

"I was saying that our friends Rhonda and Doug are celebrating their granddaughter's first birthday this weekend, and they invited us to the party. I thought it would be a great opportunity for you to meet someone else who has a child Olivia's age. Penny is just the cutest little thing, and her mom runs the *best* café in Beaumont Creek."

I didn't have to ask her which café she was talking about, given that she had talked about Rockin' Rooster nonstop since the moment I agreed to move here. Not only that, it was literally one of the few cafes in town.

"I don't know, Ma. You guys got the invite, not me. It would be rude to just show up uninvited."

"Oh, nonsense." She waved her hand dismissively before offering Olivia another bite. "It's a small town, Dominic. This is what we do. If there's a big event, everyone is invited. You won't be a bother, and I really think you'd get along great with Abby and Nate. They're a little older than you, but that doesn't mean you don't have anything in common. Plus, you both know what it's like to have a one-year-old."

"I'll think about it," I lied, having no intention of going to the party. I didn't care if it was what you did in small towns or not. It wasn't what *I* did.

"It's going to be a massive turnout," my mom continued while my dad flipped through the channels on the TV. "Abby's sister will be there—you know, Doctor Hughes? And the entire fire department will be there since Nate is the captain. Oh, and I bet we'll see some of our friends from the...."

For the second time in less than ten minutes, I stopped listening to what she was saying and focused on the one thing that lit something up inside me. Doctor Hughes would be there. Suddenly, I felt like maybe I could get on board with small-town life and join in on the festivities.

<u>Four</u>
Jane

"Where did you want me to put these balloons?" I asked as I tried to see past the massive collection that was nearly blocking my vision.

"Over by the table," Abby answered, pointing, though I could barely see which way. "Nate is over there with the guys; they'll get them set up for you."

"Got it."

I turned around, headed in the direction I assumed she meant, and prayed that I didn't come into contact with anything breakable. The kids were off with my parents, helping to finish the last-minute prep for Penny's first birthday party. I had thrown many kids' parties before in my life, but this was on another level. There were people already gathering in the park where they decided to have it, and it looked like everyone in town was going to show up.

My feet attempted to lead me in a straight line as I headed toward the table, but nothing could have prepared me for the massive body I plowed right into. Luckily, there were plenty of balloons to bounce between us, making it less of an impact.

"Oh my gosh, I'm so sorry!" I swatted the balloons out of the way and released a soft gasp as I found Dominic standing on the other side.

"It's not a problem," he laughed, the cute little dimples showing on his cheeks. "Need a hand?"

"More like twenty," I joked, shaking my head as I looked up at the tower of pink, purple, and coral-colored balloons.

"Where are you headed with them?" he asked, looking around.

I tried to pull the strings to lower them but failed miserably.

"I'm supposed to take them to my brother-in-law," I sighed. "He's at a table with the guys from the firehouse. But I seemed to have gotten turned around."

I watched his face, admiring his features, as he looked around, scanning the park until he found the table surrounded by firefighters.

"It looks like they're over there," he said, pointing. "I can walk with you. Make sure you don't take anyone else out on the way."

I felt my cheeks pulling tight as I grinned stupidly.

"Thank you, I appreciate it. I'd hate to have a balloon catastrophe on my niece's first birthday."

We walked side by side, balloons extended to the outside so I could see him, and Olivia planted firmly on his hip. He turned his head and gave me a quizzical look.

"Penny is your niece?"

I nodded.

"How do you know Penny?"

"I don't," he said, sounding nervous. "My parents are friends with her grandparents—Rhonda and Doug. They *encouraged* me to come to the party so I could meet other parents."

"Oh," I laughed. "I thought maybe you had gotten out there and started networking like you'd talked about at Olivia's appointment. Rhonda and Doug are my parents," I added, just in case he didn't already know that—which I figured he did.

He shook his head, and I could swear I saw a hint of a blush creep up his cheeks.

"I wasn't going to come today," he admitted sheepishly as we kept walking.

"Why not?"

"Because it felt weird to come to something where I didn't know anyone other than my parents. I didn't want to be an intruder."

"I wouldn't worry about that," I assured him. "I think *everyone* in town will be here today. Plus, it really is great to get out and mingle sometimes. I'm glad you decided to come."

I smiled warmly at him, feeling the butterflies swarm in my stomach when his eyes locked on mine.

"Can I be honest about something, Doctor Hughes?" he asked, his voice gruffer than a few seconds ago.

"Absolutely. And please, call me Jane." I stopped and turned toward him, giving my full attention despite the balloons that kept bopping me in the head as the gentle breeze blew them around.

"There was only one reason that I came today."

I swallowed hard, feeling the way his gaze penetrated mine.

"Oh yeah? What was it?"

"You."

A million words floated around in my head, but before I could say anything, I heard Nate calling my name.

He was beside me in a matter of seconds, taking the balloons out of my hand as the other guys helped to separate them and get them set up. I stepped back, trying to collect myself as I attempted to introduce Dominic to the guys.

The air was thick even though it was a slightly chilly day, but that was just because of the fog that Dominic had put me in. I excused myself and left him there chatting with the other guys while I went in search of Abby. If anyone knew what to do, it would be her.

I hurried through the grass, smiling at people and giving quick waves as if I were in a parade or something. Mikey and Sally were still with my parents, which left me on my own for a bit until I could gather myself.

The park felt larger than it was, and I was officially breaking a sweat as I practically ran across it to get to the tent where Abby was setting up Penny's gifts.

"Hey," she said, looking up as I brushed through. "Did you get the balloons taken care of?"

"He's here because of me," I blurted out, eyes wide and pulse racing.

Abby stopped what she was doing and tilted her head as she studied me.

"Rick?"

I pulled my head back, blinked my eyes a few times, and then shook my head.

"No," I breathed out. "Dominic. Dominic is here with Olivia."

"What? That's so awesome! I can't wait for Penny to meet her," Abby squealed and clapped her hands. "Mom told me she'd asked Darlene to bring Dominic and Olivia, but she didn't know whether they'd be able to make it. But yay! They're going to be best friends; I just know it!"

"Abby!" I snapped, feeling frustrated that she didn't see what the real problem was.

"What?"

"You didn't hear what I just said. Dominic is here because of *me*. That's what he just told me—he only came today *because of me*."

Abby sighed heavily and then let her shoulders fall.

"So, what's the problem with that?"

My eyes widened, making me look as crazy as I felt.

"You know what the problem is!" I hissed.

"I still don't think it's a problem," she laughed. "He's incredibly good-looking, so what if he's interested in you? You're single and deserve to have some fun."

I plopped down on the folding chair in the corner and rested my elbows on my knees as my head hung to my chest.

"I can't have fun with him, Abby."

"Why not?"

"Because," I groaned. "He's too young for me. Plus, he's the father of one of my patients. And my son's new teacher. There are so many reasons why this wouldn't be a good idea."

Abby sat down on the chair across from me and looked around, giving me a few minutes to calm down.

"So, why not just accept that it's a bad idea and be a naughty girl?"

I raised an eyebrow and cocked my head to the side.

"What?" She laughed and threw her hands up in the air. "I'm just saying there aren't that many guys like him in Beaumont Creek. If it were me—and I didn't have Nate—I would be all over that like white on rice."

"You're so bad," I muttered, shaking my head.

"Maybe," she shrugged. "But I've learned that life is too short to sit on the sidelines and not go after what you want. Crossing that line with Nate was one of the scariest things I've ever done, but it's also the absolute best thing. It pushed me outside of my comfort zone and showed me an entire world that I would have never known existed. Don't be so quick to rule this out just because you're scared, Jane. Like I said, you deserve to have fun, but more importantly, you deserve someone who shows up to something *just* to see *you*."

My shoulders sagged as I breathed out heavily, knowing there were some truths in what she said. While I wanted nothing more than to throw caution to the wind and explore whatever this thing was between us, I couldn't. I was a forty-two-year-old single mother with responsibilities that never stopped.

<u>Five</u>
Dominic

The party ended up being fun, and I enjoyed hanging out with Nate and the guys he worked with. Everything seemed to go well until it was time to eat. That was when they found Jones, their rookie, trying to handle the grill. They rushed over, moving him from the flames before they got any higher. I tried to hold back my laughter as they told me stories about how, after all the time they'd spent trying to teach him, he still couldn't cook to save his life.

My parents spent most of their time walking around, showing Olivia off to their friends. It didn't bother me that they stole my daughter and left me to mingle with the other adults. I was okay with that. What I wasn't okay with was watching how Jane kept avoiding me after I'd confessed that I'd come just to see her.

I knew that there was a huge chance of coming on too strong, but I couldn't help myself. There was something about her that had me feeling like I would do anything to get to spend some time with her. I didn't know her outside of the few minutes of Olivia's appointment, but that was enough for me to know that I wanted to get to know her better. That was, if she'd just let me. She'd spent the majority of the day with her sister, helping out with the party until it was time for them to do Penny's cake. Soon, everything was winding down, and people started to leave.

I was feeling frustrated, knowing that the next time I would see her would be at the parent-teacher conference next week, which would be time focused on discussing Mikey's progress, not getting to know her.

I was stalling for more time as I helped Nate and Capshaw fold up the rest of the chairs and pack them into the bed of his truck. My parents were hanging out with Jane's parents, letting Olivia and Penny play together in the grass. It was adorable, and my heart swelled at the sight of my baby girl enjoying the company of someone her own age.

"You have any plans after this?" Nate asked, giving me a nod when I looked confused as to who he was talking to.

"Nope, just taking Olivia home."

"Abby and I are having Jane and the kids over for pizza tonight. You and Olivia should join us."

My heart fluttered at the mention of Jane, and I recognized the look on Nate's face when he caught my reaction. While I'd tried not to stare at her all day, it was hard, given how she made something as simple as jeans and a t-shirt look sexy as hell.

"Umm, I'm not sure," I muttered. "But thanks for the invite."

I hated myself for being a coward and saying no, but I also hated that I had already made Jane uncomfortable earlier with my confession.

Nate stopped and leveled me with a look.

"What aren't you sure about?" he asked, arms folded over his chest.

I shrugged and ran a hand through my short hair.

"I don't know, man. I just don't want to intrude."

"You're not. You were invited."

I met his eyes, catching the way his eyebrow raised in response.

"Jane can be hard to read," he offered. "She's an incredible mother, an excellent doctor, and one of the best sisters-in-law I could ever ask for. But when she gets in her own head—she can be her own worst nightmare."

"Why are you telling me all of this?"

"Because," he sighed. "I recognize that look. And out of anyone, I know the Hughes women and how difficult they can be."

I nodded and took in his words.

"I'm not some player rushing into town, looking for the first girl to score with," I assured him.

"I know. I'd beat your ass if you were."

I felt my cheeks pinch as I grinned.

"We'll see you tonight around six. I'll text you the address."

Before I could object, he slammed the tailgate shut and hopped into the truck.

Guess I had plans for the night after all.

By the time we got home, Olivia was already asleep in her car seat. I got her inside and situated in her crib, taking the baby monitor with me while I took a quick shower. I was feeling anxious and excited about going to Nate's house tonight, but I couldn't stop the nagging feeling that he hadn't bothered to tell Jane that I would be there. I wasn't sure that it would be a surprise she would enjoy.

Images of her throughout the day overwhelmed my thoughts, and I couldn't get her off my mind if I tried. The way she'd tossed her head back and laughed at something her sister said, or how her face softened when Mikey sat next to her and curled into her side. There were so many things that she did that were so simple, yet they got under my skin in the best way possible.

I finished up and got dressed, scolding myself for spending way too long figuring out what to wear when I realized it was because I was trying to impress Jane. I decided to go with a t-shirt and jeans, matching her vibe from earlier.

By five o'clock, I was already going stir-crazy, waiting for Olivia to wake up from her nap so I could get her ready to go. I wanted to make a pit stop at the store on my way over so that we didn't show up empty-handed, but I had no idea what to take. I didn't know any of them well enough to know if they liked desserts, and if so, what kind? Nor did I know whether they were beer, wine, or hard alcohol people.

My hands were sweating as I rubbed them on my jeans, hoping the nerves would soon disappear.

Olivia woke up at the same time my phone dinged with a text message from Nate, giving me his address and directions to their house. I grinned like an idiot and rushed to get over there so I could see Jane.

We were the first to show up, which was a bit of a relief because it allowed me to get settled before Jane could see what a nervous wreck I was. I'd stopped and grabbed a six-pack of beer on my way over, along with some fudge-covered brownies I thought the kids would enjoy.

"Thank you so much for bringing these treats," Abby said, smiling as she set the dessert on the island. "I'm glad you could join us tonight."

"Thank you for the invite," I replied with a smile, holding Olivia as she tried to climb down to the floor where some of Penny's toys were scattered around.

Abby laughed and set Penny down at the same time that I put Olivia down. The girls immediately rushed over to each other, sitting side-by-side as they babbled and held toys out for each other.

"I think they're going to be best friends," Abby cooed as Nate came up behind her, wrapping his arms around her waist.

"I told you Penny needs more babies to play with," he whispered loudly.

"And now she has Olivia."

"Yeah, but imagine if she had a brother or sister," he said, wiggling his eyebrows as he tickled her sides.

"Stop it," she squealed, squirming to get away. "We have company."

I chuckled and looked down at the girls, hoping that would give them enough privacy so she would stop blushing the way she was. She looked just like Jane, and after meeting their mom Rhonda earlier, I could tell that the women in their family all looked very similar. Even Sally was taking after Jane and had the same soft angles in her face and light brown eyes.

"Fine," Nate said overly exaggeratedly. "But that doesn't mean I'm giving up that easily."

Just then, the doorbell rang, and Abby pushed away to answer it, leaving Nate and me in the living room with the girls.

"I want another baby, but she wants to wait a little longer," he offered with a shrug.

Before I could say anything, Jane walked into the living room with Mikey and Sally in front of her. Mikey gave me a huge smile and wave before giving Nate a high five and plopping down on the floor with the girls.

"Hey," Jane said, looking between Nate and me.

"Hi," I replied softly, shoving my hands into my pockets.

"The pizza should be here soon," Abby commented, sitting on the couch as Jane sat beside her.

"Want a beer?" Nate asked, reaching into the fridge and pulling out the six-pack that I had brought.

The living room and kitchen were joined together in one large space, only separated by a hallway that led to the bedrooms and bathroom.

"Sure, thank you." I walked over and took the bottle from him.

"Would you mind handing this one to Jane?" he asked with a smug smile, knowing full well what he was doing.

"No problem."

I took the other bottle and opened both before handing Jane hers.

"Thank you," she said, our fingers slightly grazing each other as she took it.

I smiled and lifted the bottle to my lips, watching hers as she did the same.

For a moment, it felt like we were the only two in the room, lost in a moment that I could live in forever. However, that was quickly interrupted by a loud shrill as Olivia started screaming.

My head whipped down, scanning the kids on the floor as I tried to figure out what had happened. I set my beer down on the coffee table and reached down to pick her up, cuddling her close as she cried harder.

"Penny!" Abby gasped, reaching over to pick her up. "You cannot hit people with your toys!"

I looked down at the bump forming on Olivia's head and then noticed the wooden block that Abby was now holding.

"I'm so sorry," Abby apologized, standing up to check on Olivia at the same time Jane stood up as well. "Is she okay?"

I gently rubbed my finger along the side of the bump, careful not to touch it.

"I think so," I murmured, feeling unsure about anything right now.

Jane's eyes found mine, and I felt the relief wash over me when she smiled and held her hands out for Olivia.

I gently passed her over, feeling my heart hammer in

my chest as Jane cuddled my daughter against her chest, shushing her with soft sounds while bouncing her on her hip.

"Did you get an owie, sweet girl?" she asked, sitting down on the couch with Olivia on her lap. She went so easily into doctor mode that I couldn't focus on anything else. But it was more than that. It wasn't just that she was a great doctor; she was also an exceptional mother. Nurturing. Caring. Giving. She was everything I could have ever wanted for my baby girl but hadn't been able to give her with her birth mother.

Olivia sat there, curled into Jane's chest as she continued to examine the bump on her head.

"She's got a bump, but it doesn't look like anything we need to be concerned with," Jane said softly, rubbing her back as her eyes flitted closed. "We'll keep an eye on her, just to be safe, but thankfully, kids are pretty tough."

"Thank you," I said sincerely.

The doorbell rang, and Abby went to get the pizza while Nate collected the kids and sent them to wash their hands before dinner. It was just Jane and I left in the room as she sat on the couch and continued to hold Olivia.

"Sorry," she laughed. "It's been so long since I've had baby cuddles; I steal them every chance I get. Just ask Abby. She's lucky Penny hasn't been in my arms from the moment we got here."

"Feel free to steal all you want; I don't mind sharing."

"She's such a sweet girl," she whispered, gently running her fingers along Olivia's hair. "You're doing a great job with her."

"Thank you," I sighed, sitting down on the couch beside her. "Most of the time, I feel like I have no idea what I'm doing."

"I don't think any of us do."

"I don't believe that for a second. You're an amazing mother and doctor. You can tell that this is all-natural for you. You're great with children."

Her cheeks flushed pink before we were called to the kitchen to join the others for dinner.

34

Six
Jane

Dinner at Abby and Nate's house was surprisingly relaxing, even after the last-minute heads-up that Dominic would be there. Abby had snuck into the bathroom to call me as soon as she knew, and we both were on to Nate trying to play matchmaker. It wasn't any surprise, given that he'd hung out with Dominic the entire time at Penny's birthday party and made sure to include him with the other guys. At first, I thought it was just Nate being Nate. He was always the good guy who made sure no one was excluded, but then I saw how he was studying me every time Dominic came near. I knew he could tell there was something there, too.

Not only that, but he had heard me freak out a handful of times to Abby. There wasn't much that I kept from Nate. He was like a brother to me, but I suddenly felt like maybe he was taking Dominic's side instead of mine. Not that anyone needed to take sides, but the last thing I needed right now was anyone *encouraging* me to explore this attraction between us. Abby was already excelling in that department, and I was starting to lose people who would convince me not to.

"Go brush your teeth, and then I'll come to say good night," I said as I got the kids inside the house. It was late, but no later than we usually got home from our weekly pizza night with Abby and Nate. Every Saturday night, we'd rotate who would host, but it had become our thing. I loved being able to hang out with them and relax for a bit. Occasionally, my parents would watch all the kids and give us an adult-only night, but those were few and far between, especially lately.

Once they were done, I headed to Sally's room first and sat down on the side of her bed to read her a story.

"Which one do you want to read tonight?" I asked, pulling my legs up underneath me as she scanned the titles on the small bookshelf beside her bed.

"This one!" She grabbed the book and handed it to me, then got under the covers and adjusted her pillow.

"*The Adventures Of Curly*, that one is your favorite, isn't it?"

She nodded and gave me a toothy grin, which made me laugh at the space where she'd recently lost another tooth.

"Alright, let's see what kind of trouble Curly gets into tonight," I whispered, kissing her forehead before I started reading.

Even though she had just turned seven, I couldn't help but think of her as my little girl who I used to rock to sleep and sing lullabies to when she was a baby. It was hard to accept that my days of cuddling babies were over unless Abby continued to have them, and I attributed it to being one step closer to that *next step* in my life, where things would change even more.

I focused on the words and tuned out the rush of emotions that were overwhelming me. After a few chapters, the soft sound of her snoring filled the room. I put the book back on the bookshelf, tucked her in, and kissed her goodnight before sneaking out of the room and closing the door behind me.

Mikey's door was closed, so I knocked lightly, waiting for him to invite me in before opening the door. Things felt harder with him these days, more strained than they were before. I wasn't sure if it was because he was getting closer to being a teenager or if nine was just a rough age for boys. Either way, I found myself treading lightly when I could to avoid more conflict. There had been a lot of change over the past few months with his dad proposing to his girlfriend. She was twenty years younger than him and barely even legal, which meant that the kids had been spending less time with him as he worked to get his new life started.

"Come in," he answered loud enough for me to hear but not loud enough to wake his sister.

I turned the knob and opened the door, smiling when I saw him sitting on his bed, looking at a book Nate had recently bought for him. Mikey was suddenly into technology and figuring out how things worked, so Nate had encouraged that curiosity by taking him shopping at the local bookstore. I don't know if I was more impressed with his interest in something other than setting things on fire or that Nate got him to sit down and willingly look at a book.

"Whatcha reading?" I asked, sitting on the edge of his bed.

"Nothing," he said, snapping the book shut and sliding it into his nightstand drawer.

My brows pinched together in a frown, but I forced it away, not wanting him to see my disappointment.

"Oh, okay."

We sat there for a few minutes in this awkward silence that I hated.

"Did you have fun at Penny's party?" I asked, hoping to change the subject quickly.

"Yeah. It was more for little kids, though."

"Well, it was *her* birthday party," I laughed.

The corners of his lips turned up into a smile that I had missed recently.

"I was thinking maybe we could go fishing tomorrow," I said easily, trying to gauge his reaction. "Do something fun before you guys go camping with Nana and Pop for spring break."

Technically, they still had one week left of school before spring break started, but I was desperate to spend as much time with them as I could before then. Something gnawed at me, making me sad that I wasn't going to be able to go camping with them, missing out on the fun they would have.

"But you don't like fishing," he objected with a scowl.

"Yes, I do," I laughed, gently elbowing him as I scooted closer.

"Then why do you always make that face when you catch a fish?"

"Because they stink." My cheeks hurt from how hard I was grinning. "Just like you when we get home from a day of fishing," I teased.

"You're not supposed to sniff them, mom." He rolled his eyes, the smile still prominent on his cute little face.

"I'll make a note of it. So, do you wanna go?"

"Sure," he shrugged.

Sundays were usually my day to get the chores done around the house, but with them being gone for a week soon, I wanted to squeeze in as much fun time as possible. Plus, the weather was supposed to be beautiful tomorrow, and we could all use the fresh air.

"Alright, we'll go to the store in the morning and grab what we need. But you better get some rest, or you're going to be too tired, and I'll end up out-fishing you again." I raised my eyebrows and gave him my best competitive look.

"No way," he said, returning the look.

"Oh, it's on," I teased, reaching over and tickling him. Though I knew it would only be tolerated for a few seconds before he realized he was *too old* for it and begged me to stop.

"Bring it, *grandma*," he shot back, laughing hysterically as I dug my fingers in deeper.

"*Grandma? Grandma?* Oh, those are fighting words!"

He continued squirming and laughing until I gave in and let him go. I stood up and placed my hands on my hips, staring down at him and wondering where my little boy who loved firetrucks and mommy cuddles went.

"Get some sleep, pal. You're gonna need it."

He winked and climbed under the covers, getting situated while I waited. I kissed his forehead and told him goodnight before turning off the light and closing the door behind me.

It was late, but not late enough for me to be ready to go to sleep. My brain was still super active, my thoughts going a mile a minute, mostly about Dominic and sweet Olivia. I felt bad for her with the decent-sized bump she got from Penny hitting her with a wooden block, but thankfully, she seemed to be doing okay. I'd kept an eye on her throughout the night until everyone called it a night and went home.

I curled up on the couch, flipping through the channels on the TV, when my phone suddenly started ringing. I reached for it from the coffee table and checked the caller ID, wondering who would call this late.

Seeing the phone number for the hospital, I immediately answered and held the phone to my ear.

"Hello?"

"Hi, Doctor Hughes, I'm sorry to bother you, but we have a pediatric patient of yours who was just brought in. Her father said that she had been hit in the head earlier in the evening and then began vomiting shortly after he got home. We wanted to check in with you as he said that you had examined her after it first happened. Are you able to come down?"

My heart sank in my chest as I held my hand to it.

"Yes, I'll be there shortly."

I hung up and then called my mother while I grabbed my purse and waited for her to get there. It wasn't often that I got a call from the hospital regarding one of my patients, but it happened occasionally. Thankfully, my parents lived close enough that they could come by to watch the kids while I went in.

Ten minutes later, I was out the door and on my way to

Dominic and Olivia. Once I got to the hospital, I found them sitting in one of the exam rooms with a nurse checking Olivia's vitals. She was screaming at the top of her lungs, her little face red and splotchy.

The moment she saw me, her hands reached out, and I took her.

"Oh, my sweet girl," I said calmly, holding her to my chest. "What's going on?"

Before Dominic could answer, Olivia threw up all over my chest.

He covered his face with his hands and grimaced.

"Don't worry about it," I assured him before looking at the nurse. "Can you please grab me a pair of scrubs, size medium?"

She nodded and slipped out, pulling the curtain closed behind her.

"How long has she been throwing up?" I asked, not bothering to clean myself up as I continued to hold and comfort her.

He looked down at his watch, worry evident on his face.

"About an hour, off and on. I brought her in as soon as it started since she still had the bump on her head. I remembered vomiting as a warning sign with head injuries and didn't want to overlook it."

"You did the right thing. Don't worry; we'll figure out what's going on. Has she had anything to eat or drink after you left Nate and Abby's?"

Now that Olivia was calm, I sat her on the exam table and looked at the bump on her head. It was still red and a little swollen, but I was pretty confident that it wasn't the reason she was sick.

"Nope. She fell asleep on the way home, so I transferred her to her crib as soon as we got inside. Then she woke up like this."

"Okay," I replied, offering him a smile before checking her pupils. I lifted my finger and made tickling motions, getting her eyes to follow it.

A few minutes later, the nurse returned with the scrubs I'd asked for and the items I would need to do a complete exam.

Dominic sat in the chair in the corner, watching as the nurse and I worked through checking Olivia. She was alert and focused, which made me think maybe she was dehydrated from being in the sun for too long. That, combined with junk food at Nate and Abby's house, would give a lot of kids a stomachache.

"How often does she eat sweets or junk food?" I asked, holding my stethoscope to her back and then moving it down.

"Not often. I eat pretty clean, so I feed her the same."

I smiled at Olivia, who was playing with the tongue depressor the nurse had given her to distract her while we were examining her.

"From what I can see, she looks fine," I said softly. "If I had to guess why she's throwing up, it would be a combination of excess junk food, which her body isn't used to, and possibly some dehydration from spending so much time outside today."

His lips pursed into an O as he released a heavy breath.

"So, she's okay?"

"She's okay," I nodded. "I recommend giving her some Pedialyte to replenish the fluids she's lost, but other than that, she should be just fine. Hopefully, it's out of her system. Getting her hydrated will help, and then maybe some crackers or bland food to settle her stomach."

"Okay, I can do that. Thank you so much; I appreciate you coming down to check on her. Sorry to pull you away from home on a Saturday night."

"It's nothing," I said, waving my hand in the air. "Do you have a change of clothes for her?"

"Yeah, I think I have some pajamas for her in the diaper bag."

I played with Olivia while he grabbed them, along with a clean diaper. Then I stepped out into the bathroom, changed my clothes, and tossed my dirty ones in the bag the nurse had given me. When I went back into the room, he was finishing zipping up her coat, and I felt my ovaries flutter. *Stupid baby fever*.

"The nurse should be in soon with the paperwork to get you guys out of here, but if you need anything tonight, please call my cell. I'm happy to go by and check on her again," I offered, handing him a piece of paper on which I'd written my info.

"Thank you," he said, his fingers brushing mine for the second time tonight and causing the same electrical reaction as the first time. "Can I take you and the kids out to lunch tomorrow?"

I opened my mouth to speak but snapped it shut when I saw the panic in his eyes.

"Sorry, that was rather forward of me, wasn't it? I just meant that I wanted to express my gratitude for what you did for me tonight."

"I appreciate it, really. I'm actually taking the kids fishing tomorrow, but thank you for the offer."

"Oh, okay." He nodded his head, but I could see the disappointment on his face.

"Maybe a raincheck for another time?" *I suggested, instantly kicking myself for it. What the hell was I doing? I was supposed to be keeping my distance from him, not taking him up on offers to go to lunch with my kids and me.*

"Absolutely. Just let me know when."

I smiled and felt the butterflies go crazy in my stomach again. Dominic was a temptation that I didn't need right now, but that didn't stop me from wanting him in a way that I shouldn't.

<u>Seven</u>
Dominic

Last night, I didn't sleep a wink. After we left the hospital, I got Olivia home and gave her a quick bath before getting her down for the night. Luckily, I had some Pedialyte on hand from when she had been sick a few weeks ago and was able to get her to drink some.

She had given me quite a scare, and while I trusted the ER staff to know how to care for her, I couldn't deny the overwhelming relief I felt the moment I saw Jane. It also didn't go unnoticed how my daughter continued to gravitate to her every chance that she had. Though, in all fairness, I couldn't blame her. Jane had the same pull with me, and I found myself being drawn to her, whether I wanted to or not.

I'd slept in Olivia's room on the floor beside her crib. Knowing that I was right there if she needed anything was the reassurance that I needed. My mother had offered to come over and help after I gave her the update that we were home, but I politely declined and promised her I would call if we needed anything.

By morning, Olivia woke up bright-eyed and bubbly, just like her normal self. I, on the other hand, was exhausted and wanted nothing more than to crawl into bed and sleep the day away. But, it was Sunday, and I couldn't afford to do that. There were chores to get done, homework to grade, and time that I wanted to spend with my daughter.

When I went into the kitchen to make breakfast, I frowned when I realized that the milk had expired. I checked the other gallon, and that one was sour as well. I scrubbed a hand down my face and groaned, knowing that I was heading to the grocery store before the day officially got started.

"You wanna go shopping?" I asked Olivia as she reached for me from her Pack 'N Play.

She giggled as I picked her up and gently tickled her sides.

Fifteen minutes later, we headed through the aisles, grabbing the stuff we'd need for the week. At least I was getting this out of the way now, which would free up my afternoon.

I pushed the cart around the corner, laughing as Olivia played with a bag of noodles, trying to get them open.

Just then, I came to an abrupt stop, just barely missing hitting Jane's cart with mine.

"Oh, sorry!" she apologized, pulling her cart out of the way before looking up to see who it was that she had almost run into.

"I'm starting to think you've got it out for me," I joked. "You seem to try to take me out every chance you get. First with balloons, now with groceries."

She smiled, and I noticed the faint blush that crept up her cheeks.

"I'm so sorry about that," she laughed. "I am distracted this morning, apparently."

"It's not a problem; I was just teasing."

Olivia turned as far as she could in the seat and reached for Jane.

"Good morning. How are you feeling today?" Jane asked, reaching forward and offering Olivia her hand, which Olivia immediately wrapped her fingers around.

"She's doing a lot better," I answered. "She hasn't gotten sick since last night when she…"

I let my sentence fade, knowing I didn't need to remind her that my daughter had thrown up on her.

"That's good; I'm happy to hear that."

"Can we get Cheetos?"

I looked past Jane to see Sally and Mikey coming around the corner, bags of chips tightly tucked in their arms.

Jane's eyebrows rose as she looked at the contents.

"It's just a day of fishing, you guys," she laughed. "I don't know that we need *that much* junk food."

"But daddy said that fish like Cheetos," Sally countered, holding the bag up.

Jane tilted her head to the side, calling her daughter on the BS she was feeding her.

"He did!" Sally exclaimed, stomping her foot.

I bit the inside of my cheek to keep from laughing.

"Dad really said it, mom," Mikey added, looking from Sally to Jane.

She sighed heavily.

"I can personally vouch for the Cheetos bait," I said softly, pulling my lower lip between my bottom teeth.

She covered her face in her hands and pretended to mumble some choice curse words.

"Not you, too," she joked. "You're supposed to be on my side."

I shrugged.

"What can I say? Fish love Cheetos."

She pursed her lips together and narrowed her eyes as she looked between us.

"I feel like you're all playing me here," she sighed. "But I don't want to be the reason why we don't catch anything today, so I'll allow it this time."

"I don't think that's going to be the reason why you don't catch anything," Mikey said with a huge grin that spread tightly across his face.

"Oh yeah? Then why is it you think I won't catch any fish?" She planted her hand on her hips, her smile matching his.

"Because *I'm* going to catch all of them. There won't be any left for you."

She raised an eyebrow and wagged her finger at him.

"Oh, it's on," she laughed.

I felt myself smiling, enjoying their playful banter. Part of me wished I had someone to share that with, and I hoped Olivia would still be close to me when she got older.

"Sounds like quite the competition, I can't wait to hear who the winner is," I said, holding onto the handle of the cart as Olivia played with my fingers. I smiled down at her, thankful she was feeling better.

"Why don't you come with us?" Mikey offered, surprising both Jane and me.

It was my turn to raise my eyebrows, unsure how to respond to him.

Jane's face flushed that cute shade of red again, and I could tell she was struggling with what to say. Probably thinking of a way to let me down easily.

"Oh, thanks for the offer, but Olivia and I have some more errands we need to run."

Mikey's face fell, and I noticed a bit of disappointment on Sally's as well. Jane's shoulders dropped, and I could tell she didn't want them to be upset. But inviting someone to a special day you had planned with your kids shouldn't be something you feel obligated to do.

"Okay," Mikey said softly, tossing the stuff from his arms into the shopping cart.

"Maybe another time," Sally added, still holding onto the bag of Cheetos.

My heart squeezed inside of my chest, tightening with the hurt looks that they continued to wear.

"We wouldn't mind the company," Jane said, lifting her eyes to mine. "If you guys would like to join us."

My palms started sweating as I gripped the handle harder. I wanted nothing more than to spend time with Jane, but I didn't want to intrude on their time together.

"I don't want to overstep," I replied softly, hoping she would read between the lines and understand what I was trying to say without having to go into more detail.

"You're not," she assured me. "Besides, I need someone to help me out fish Mikey."

She winked playfully, making sure Mikey saw.

"Um, alright," I laughed nervously. While I wanted nothing more than to join them, I was also suddenly very aware that I would be spending time one on one with just Jane and her kids. It felt almost like a date, a chance for our families to get to know each other. "If you're really sure."

"I am. We would love to have you guys join us."

"Thank you. I'll have to run some stuff home, but can meet you guys there if that works?"

"We don't mind waiting for you," Jane said. "We like to go to a hidden spot, so I don't want you to get lost. And since you have some more shopping to do, I'll go ahead and do mine real quick, and then we can meet at my place when you're ready."

"Okay, sounds good. What all do I need to take?"

I wasn't sure how long we would be there or what the plan was, so I didn't want to look like an ass and show up empty-handed, using the supplies she bought.

"We have rods and all of that stuff, but if you want anything special for you or Olivia, feel free to take that. I always pack sandwiches for lunch and snacks for the day. Plus drinks. But I've already got all of that covered."

"Alright, I'll think of something I can contribute," I said, my brain already going a mile a minute. "Unless you want to take me up on my offer to take you guys out for lunch?"

I knew I shouldn't have said it in front of the kids, but my mouth moved faster than my brain.

"No pressure," I added quickly. "Just thought I would throw it out there."

Jane looked from me to her kids, noticing the excitement in their eyes.

"Sure, that sounds wonderful. Thank you."

"Okay. I won't be too long. Meet you at your house in half an hour?"

"Perfect. I'll text you the address."

I nodded and grinned like an idiot before pushing the cart away and trying to remember what I had come to the store for in the first place. Today was a surprising change of events, but I didn't mind in the least.

Eight

Jane

I hurried through the store, grabbing what we needed for the week so that we wouldn't have to rush through fishing. It was still early in the day, but it felt like it exploded after Mikey invited Dominic and Olivia to come fishing with us.

It wasn't that I didn't want them to come; I was just so blindsided by the offer that I didn't know what to do. I could tell that Dominic was trying to give me an out, but I couldn't bring myself to accept it when I saw the look on Mikey's face. Part of me wondered if he missed having a guy—someone other than my dad—to fish with. Rick didn't bother to do stuff like that with the kids anymore, and it seemed to affect Mikey more than it did Sally.

After unloading the groceries and packing up what we needed for fishing, I got a text from Dominic that he was on his way and would be there in ten minutes. I piled the kids into the SUV and waited until I saw him pull up. I waved at Dominic to let him know we were heading out. He waved back, looking ridiculously sexy in his truck. *Why was that even a thing I was thinking about right now?*

It was an hour's drive to the fishing spot, so I took advantage of putting a movie on the rear-mounted DVD players for the kids and popped an earbud in so I could call Abby and talk to her about what had happened.

The movie was loud enough to distract them from my conversation and grabbed their attention right away. I waited until I was on the highway before pressing send on my phone. After a few rings, Abby answered.

"Hey, sis, what's up?"

"Dominic is going fishing with us," I said quietly, through gritted teeth.

"Okay, is that code word for something?" I could hear the laughter in her voice and a slight echo, knowing she had me on speakerphone.

"No! Like he's in his truck behind me as we speak. Mikey invited him, and he accepted!"

"He's taking you from behind?" Abby giggled. "Fun."

I blew out a frustrated breath.

"Abby. Get it together and focus! This is a big problem."

"Oh, so he's *big*. And taking you from behind before he goes fishing. Is that like a code word for him going down on you?" She paused for a moment while I rolled my eyes. It was better just to let her get it out of her system. "Eeeww. Gross. I don't think I'd want a guy comparing oral sex with me to fishing. Did you shower?"

"Why couldn't God give me a sister who actually listens?" I asked playfully, though I kinda wanted to punch her in the boob. Maybe I had watched Mean Girls a few too many times recently.

"Because you got one that encourages you to *take the bait*."

"What are you talking about?" I asked, feeling slightly confused but more irritated.

"Is he trying to *reel her in?*" Nate asked, joining in on the conversation.

"Ah, fishing puns. Clever."

I kept my hands tightly wrapped around the steering wheel, checking the rear-view mirror to make sure Dominic was still behind me.

"Yeah, but she doesn't want to take his *bait*," Abby said to Nate.

"I don't know; I think he was *snagged* at the sight of her," Nate added.

"She caught him like a fish with a hook in its mouth—though I have a feeling she wants something else in her mouth instead." Abby snorted, thoroughly enjoying herself.

"Are you two done?" I asked impatiently. "Cause I have a real problem."

"Oh, a *reel* problem. Like maybe he can't *cast* it good enough?"

"Don't worry, Jane, you could *school* him if you have to."

I sighed heavily, trying not to laugh at how corny they were being.

"You. Guys," I groaned. "Are you going to help me or not?"

"I don't know," Abby said. "I think she's a goner."

"Hook, line, and sinker," Nate agreed.

"Alright. That's it. I'm hanging up and calling someone else," I threatened, though we all knew I had no one to call.

"What?" Abby laughed. "I saw a great *oppor-tuna-ty*."

"Okay, I'm hanging up!"

I was about to press the end button when I heard Abby squeal.

"Don't be so dramatic, we're just teasing. Hold on for a second."

I could hear her whispering something to Nate as she took me off speakerphone.

"Yes, I promise you can go deep sea diving as soon as I'm off the phone. Now go; Jane needs me."

"I didn't need to hear that," I muttered.

"Sorry, all those puns got him worked up, and you know how that goes."

I shook my head to clear the thoughts of Abby and Nate doing God knows what when she was done with our call.

"Alright, so what's the problem?" she asked, all traces of humor gone from her tone. "Did you not want him to go?"

"I don't know," I whispered, looking in the mirror to see Mikey watching me. "It's not necessarily that; I was just surprised, is all."

"Did he seem like he wanted to go, or was it more like he felt obligated to since Mikey invited him?"

"Honestly, I'm not sure. He seemed nervous, so I feel like maybe there was some guilt tied into it." I turned my head and lowered my voice, even though Mikey had returned his attention back to the movie.

"Well, I wouldn't worry too much. It's not like it's a one-on-one date or something. You guys are going fishing with your kids. Nothing romantic is going to happen with three little cock-blockers hanging around."

"Abby!" I gasped, surprised to hear her talk like that.

"What? It's true. Trust me; we feel the effect of not being able to do what we want when we want, thanks to little miss Penny. There have been plenty of times where we've started something, only to have her interrupt before we get to the good part."

"Still, I didn't expect to hear that from you."

"Yeah, well, Nate has been obsessively trying to knock me up again, so it's all that's on my mind these days."

"Did you decide you want to try again? I thought you wanted to wait a little bit longer?"

"I do, but at the same time, I'm not getting any younger. I worry that if we don't have another one soon, I'll miss any chance I might have."

"There's still time," I tried to reassure her.

"Easy for you to say. You already have your babies," she laughed.

I let my shoulders fall heavily. I knew that I was done having kids, but that still hadn't done anything to ease the ache that I felt when I thought about not having another baby.

"But back to your problem—so you're going fishing with Dominic and Mikey invited him. I really don't think it's anything to worry about unless you're finally willing to talk about the lust you've been harboring for him but refuse to admit."

"I'm not lusting after him," I hissed out, hoping that neither of the kids heard me.

"You totally are. This is worse than you were with Capshaw."

"There was nothing going on between us, and you guys made it a big deal, anyway."

"Jane, you were sneaking him over for late-night booty calls—that's a big deal for you. Plus, we had to give you shit about it because you weren't willing to tell us about it. It wasn't until Nate had to drop something off at your house and found Capshaw's truck in your driveway that we knew what was happening. At least this time, you could just come clean from the start and admit that you're into Dominic."

"I'm not into him," I argued, though I knew it was pointless. Abby knew me better than anyone, so she already knew the truth.

"Maybe not, but you still wouldn't be complaining if he was in you."

"Abby!" I felt my cheeks blush.

"It's true, and you know it."

"You know that's not helpful at all, right? I called you for a reason."

"Yeah, but I'm not going to sit here and agree with you that this is some big disaster in the making. What's the worst that happens? Your kids enjoy a day fishing with a nice guy that happens to be interested in their mom? He's a good guy, Jane. It's not like you're going with a serial killer, and we have to go search the lake for pieces of your body when you guys are done."

"What if they get attached to them? What am I supposed to do then?"

"Them?"

"It's not just Dominic, Abby. What if they fall in love with Olivia like I…"

I swallowed hard, refusing to allow the words out of my mouth.

"Oh, Jane," she whispered. "You already fell in love with his daughter, didn't you?"

"I love all kids; that's why I'm a pediatrician."

"No," she countered. "This one is different. Olivia is the reason you don't want to let your guard down with Dominic. You're afraid that if things don't work out between you guys, you won't just lose him, you'll lose her too."

I pulled off the exit we needed to take and slowed down as I came to a stop sign.

"She's not mine to lose." I sucked in a deep breath and then took the turn that I needed. "We're almost there; I gotta go."

I hung up before she could say anything else. I knew it was childish, but my heart couldn't risk hearing the truth in her words.

Nine
Dominic

"Thanks for your help, Mikey," I said with a smile as he pulled the other side of the Pack 'N Play down. I'd grabbed it at the last minute, knowing it would come in handy today with Olivia. On top of that, I packed a few of her favorite toys, snacks, drinks, and a few changes of clothes since I wasn't sure what the weather would be like at the lake.

"No problem."

I finished putting Olivia's toys in with her while he ran off to check on Jane, who was busy setting up the rods. I'd caught a glimpse of her a handful of times and found myself easily distracted by how great her ass looked in the tight black leggings she was wearing with the hoodie that would look great thrown on my floor as I devoured her body.

It was chilly but not too cold, so I left Olivia in the sweats she was wearing and tossed her favorite blanket in the Pack 'N Play with her. She was already distracted with her toys, so I took a few minutes to go see if I could help Jane.

"Need a hand?" I offered, grinning when I saw her trying to put a Cheetos puff on the hook.

"I blame you for this," she teased, narrowing her eyes at me as she passed me the rod and bag of Cheetos.

"Hey, I'll take it," I laughed. "But you'll be singing me praises when Mikey catches a ton of fish today."

"I thought you were supposed to be on *my* side. Don't you mean when *I* catch a ton of fish?"

"Nope, no way. I've gotta get in Mikey's good graces."

"And why is that?" she asked, leaning back on her hands, her body looking amazing on the boulder she was sitting on.

"Because us dudes have to stick together. Look around you; I'm easily outnumbered here," I joked, nodding to her, Sally, and Olivia. "Mikey is my only chance at staying sane with all of these girls around."

"Mmm hmm." She pressed her lips together and tried not to smile.

"Plus, how else am I supposed to try to impress you, if not with my badass fish-catching skills?"

A soft pink blush crept up her neck and onto her cheeks, making it one of my favorite things about her. I knew it was risky to keep coming on to her, but at the same time, the way she reacted when I did made me feel like maybe this wasn't one-sided after all.

She opened her mouth to say something but was quickly interrupted by Sally.

"Is my fishing rod ready yet?"

"Not yet, sweetie. Dominic is helping me, so it should only be a few more minutes."

"Okay!"

I focused on getting the Cheetos puff on the hook and then handed the rod to Jane before taking the next one and getting it set up. Within a few minutes, they were all ready, and I watched as Mikey and Sally cast their lines into the water.

I checked on Olivia, making sure she was still good before I leaned next to Jane and gently bumped her with my shoulder.

"You know you can't out fish Mikey if you don't actually put your line in the water?"

"I know," she laughed, but made no effort to reach for the rod beside her.

"Mom hates casting," Mikey offered, keeping his attention on the water as he nudged his sister and pointed to the bubbles on the surface of the water.

"You hate casting?" I asked, lowering my voice.

She rolled her eyes and grabbed the rod.

"Out of everything fishing related, it's one of my least favorite things."

"What's the other?"

"Taking the fish off the hook," Sally said, smiling at us over her shoulder.

"Fishing used to be something they did with their dad," Jane said softly. "Before we got divorced, we'd come out here together as a family. Rick, my ex-husband, would handle all of that stuff. I was never any good at it, but once he stopped wanting to do it, I took over. It's never been quite the same, no matter how hard I try."

My heart pulled tightly in my chest by her words. I didn't

know her ex, but I already hated him.

"Would you like me to teach you?" I offered.

"Oh no, that's okay. It's really not necessary," she rushed out, her cheeks turning red again.

"I don't mind. It's easy once you get the hang of it."

She chewed her lower lip while she thought about it. I noticed how she looked at Mikey and Sally, who both had their backs to us as they waited to catch something.

"Let him teach you, mommy. That way, you can know for next time," Sally said softly.

"Yeah, you're always telling us that it's good to learn something new," Mikey added.

I grinned cheekily as she shook her head and covered her face with her hands.

"You're going to see how much I suck," she laughed.

Her words might have had innocent intentions, but they still shot straight to my cock, forcing me to discreetly adjust my jeans before it became obvious what had happened.

She seemed to realize the weight of her words at the same time because she lowered her hands, covered her mouth, and turned beat red as her eyes nearly bulged out of her head.

"I didn't mean—"

I held my hand up to stop her before she could ramble on and further embarrass herself.

"Why don't you grab my rod, and we'll get started."

Fuck.

I closed my eyes and pinched the bridge of my nose, hoping she hadn't caught the error in my sentence. It was as if she was rubbing off on me in the worst possible way.

Her eyes lit up, and a small snort escaped her lips.

I stepped closer to her, reaching around her to grab a fishing rod.

"Now I blame *you* for this," I teased, letting my breath graze gently across her ear. "You've got me jumbling my words and saying things that sound worse than I intended."

"Hey, you seem to have the same effect on me," she laughed. "I guess neither of us could get our words out if we tried."

There were so many things that I wanted to say, but now wasn't the time or place.

"Alright, let's teach you how to cast like a pro," I said, effectively changing the subject.

She stood up and joined me by the edge, next to the kids. I checked on Olivia again, smiling as she giggled and played with her toys. She was such a calm baby and so easily entertained that I often wondered what I did to deserve such a blessing.

Once Jane was standing in front of me, I handed her the fishing pole and stood behind her as I guided her hands with mine. I felt the way my body instantly reacted to hers, the need to touch her intensifying by the second.

"Okay," I said, my voice gruff. "Hold your hand up here, and then place the other right below. You're going to use your bottom one to hold on to the pole and the one on top to press this button to release the line."

"Okay," she breathed heavily, making my cock twitch in my jeans.

"You ready?"

She nodded but didn't say anything.

"Pull your arms back like this," I guided, helping her through the motion. "And then release."

She did as instructed and squealed when the line sailed through the air before plunging into the water.

"Oh my God! I did it!"

She turned and faced me, a beautiful grin spread across her face. Before I knew what was happening, she reached forward and pulled me into her for a hug.

"Thank you so much," she said, still holding onto me.

I wrapped my hand around her waist, hugging her back.

"My pleasure," I replied, meaning every damn word.

Ten

Jane

"Alright, what's the final count?" I asked, holding my pen over the notepad as Dominic counted the fish we'd caught throughout the day. Olivia held onto me tightly, napping peacefully as Mikey and Sally ate a snack at the picnic table.

"Mikey six, Sally four, and you five," he paused and then looked up at me with a smug smirk that showed off those sexy dimples. "And I finished with eight."

"Eight?!" I exclaimed. "How is that possible?"

"Well, once you made this a competition, I had no choice but to take you down."

I shook my head and laughed, knowing that I was going to regret it after I put the offer out there this morning. After seeing how much fun the kids were having and how easily Dominic and Olivia seemed to mesh in with us, I decided it would be fun to have a friendly competition. The winner got to plan a fun outing for all five of us after the kids got back from spring break.

"I knew better than to trust you," I teased, shaking my finger at him.

"I told you I was good," he shrugged. "You just didn't want to believe me."

Oh, I wanted to believe him, but my body was trying to convince me he was good at other things too. I desperately wanted to see if I was right.

"Well, since you seem to be so good at fishing, maybe you have ideas of what to do with all of this," I said, pointing to the pile on the tarp at his feet.

"Maybe we can take some to dad?" Mikey said, the hope in his voice that broke my heart.

"Sure, we can do that," I replied, trying to keep the strain out of my voice. "I'll call him when we're done and see if we can drop them off."

"Maybe Nana and Pop want some, too?" Sally added.

"That's an excellent suggestion, but I think they're stocked up from last weekend. Plus, you know Pop is going to catch more next week when you guys go camping."

I shifted Olivia, making sure she could still easily breathe after she had nuzzled her face further between my boobs. Dominic's eyes followed her movement, then moved to my chest. I felt the heat flame in my cheeks when he looked up and found me watching him.

Soon, I wasn't the only one who was blushing as he quickly looked away and packed up the fish.

"If you want me to clean these before we go, I can," he offered.

"It's up to you. The kids are still snacking, and Olivia is sleeping pretty good, so I'm not in a rush if you're not."

"Sounds like a plan. I'll go ahead and package some up for their dad. How many do you want for him?"

I shrugged. I had no idea whether Rick would even take the time to cook what we dropped off, but I didn't want the kids to have any more disappointment than necessary. I also didn't know if his fiancé ate fish, given that we barely knew anything about her.

"Maybe two or three?"

He nodded and then pulled a knife out and began cleaning them.

"How many do you want?" he asked a few minutes later, looking up at me.

"Go ahead and take what you want first. The kids will be gone with my parents next week, and I really don't want to freeze it, nor do I plan to cook much. I can see if Abby and Nate want whatever is left over."

Suddenly, he stopped what he was doing and stood in front of me, tilting his head to the side as he studied my face.

"You're not going to cook while they're gone?"

"Probably not," I laughed nervously, feeling the weight of his gaze lingering on me. "I eat a lot of salads, so that's what I usually do when they're gone."

He shoved a hand through his hair and then looked me in the eye.

"Alright, how about we make a deal?"

"I don't know; I think I lost enough for today," I joked.

He shook his head and closed his eyes.

"The deal is that you make the salad, I'll cook the rest of

the meal. You'll join Olivia and me for dinner while the kids are gone next week."

I pulled my head back, surprised by him.

"What? No, you're crazy. You don't have to feed me. I'm a grown woman, fully capable of—"

He stepped closer, invading my space, and pressed a finger to my lips.

"Jane, I have no doubt you can take care of yourself. I would like your company, and if I'm cooking for myself, why not cook for you too? We can enjoy a few meals together unless you really don't want to."

My heart hammered in my chest, my lips still tingling from his touch.

"You don't have to do that," I whispered.

"I know. I want to. So, do we have a deal? You bring the salad, I'll make some fried catfish since we have plenty to use."

Before I could overthink it or talk myself out of it, I let the word *yes* tumble from my mouth, earning another dimpled smile from Dominic.

By the time we got everything packed up and loaded into the vehicles, it was late. Dominic still wanted to treat us to dinner, but we came to the compromise of getting takeout instead of trying to go sit down at a restaurant. The kids had school tomorrow, which meant we would need to get them showered and to bed at a decent time.

Dominic agreed to drop some of the catfish we caught to Nate and Abby before he picked up dinner at Surf 'N Shack while I took the kids by their dad's house. I'd called Rick once we got on the road, and though he didn't sound happy to hear from me, his tone shifted when he heard the kids speak and knew that he was on speakerphone.

Thankfully, it was a quick stop since he was in a shitty mood. Mikey asked him about coming to the parent-teacher conference this week, but Rick was already giving him a reason why he couldn't go before he knew what day it was. By the time we got to the house, my head was pounding with a headache that I thought I had divorced a few years ago.

The kids were organizing their backpacks for school when the doorbell rang. "Finish up, so we can eat," I said, as I opened up the front door to find Dominic looking absolutely delicious. He was somehow balancing Olivia on one hip and bags of groceries on the other.

"Hey, let me help you with that," I offered, reaching for the bags. Instead, Olivia held her hands out for me, so Dominic shifted so I could take her.

My heart melted every time she did that, and I found myself falling more and more in love with this sweet girl. I closed the door and locked it, then followed him into the kitchen, where he was setting the bags down on the table. A few minutes later, Sally and Mikey joined us, excited to see Dominic and Olivia again, even though it had only been a few hours since we'd all been together.

We sat down and ate together, the sound of laughter filling the room and creating a new longing deep inside. I wanted this—all of this. I wanted a complete family again, and the way Dominic was looking at me made me think that maybe he did, too.

Eleven

Jane

"How was fishing yesterday?" Abby asked as she prepared my skinny vanilla latte.

I stopped by Rockin' Rooster every morning before work when I had the time, which was my treat to myself after dropping the kids off at school. Some days we had our shit together, and I got my morning treat; other days, we were all running around like chickens with our heads cut off, and I was stuck with the coffee at the clinic.

"It was fun," I said, taking a sip as soon as she handed me the to-go cup. I also wanted to be distracted so I didn't have to answer the question she was really asking based on the look she was giving me.

"Fun? Like he *reeled you in* fun?"

I rolled my eyes and took another drink.

"Funny," I said sarcastically. "You better stop with all of these silly puns, or we're never going to be able to talk to dad about fishing again."

"True. But I can't miss an opportunity to tease you," she laughed. "Have you talked to him since yesterday?"

I shifted my weight and scooted to the end of the counter so the woman who had just walked in could look in the display case.

"Not since last night."

"Last night?" she questioned with a raised eyebrow.

"After dinner."

"You guys had dinner together?" she whispered loudly. The door opened, and the old rooster let out a strangled sounding crowing noise from above it.

"You need to get that thing fixed," I said, nodding to the antique Rooster that had been in our family since my grandparents owned Rockin' Rooster before they passed it down to my sister. I quickly averted my eyes, as Capshaw, Nate, and the other guys from the firehouse walked inside.

"I know. It's on my list of things to do."

I stood off to the side while Abby and Sherry tended to the customers. I still had time before I had to get to work, which was usually the only time Abby and I got for some private sister talk. Though this morning was busier than usual, so it didn't look like that was going to happen.

I looked down at my watch, checking the time while debating whether to go to work early or hang out for a few more minutes while Abby cleared the line.

"What time is Mikey's parent-teacher conference?" Abby asked as she came around to the other counter to prepare the to-go coffee orders while Sherry wrapped pastries and packaged them.

"This afternoon. I'm leaving work early to get there for Sally's, and then I have Mikey's right after."

"Is Rick going too?"

"Does he ever go?" I asked sarcastically.

"True."

"Hey, Abby, I'm going to crank out a batch of cinnamon rolls for the guys. Do you mind taking over up front?" Sherry asked, nodding to the firefighters behind her.

"Nope, I've got it covered. Thanks, Sherry." She smiled at her assistant manager before heading to the register, where Nate was waiting for her with his lips pursed for a kiss.

"Come on, man, no one wants to see that," Capshaw muttered, glancing briefly in my direction.

"Well then, blame Jones. He's the one who burned breakfast, so we all had to come here for reinforcements. I can't be this close to my wife and not kiss her."

I looked over at Jones, who was turning an adorable shade of red as he rubbed a hand across his neck.

"Aww, poor Jones. I can give you some cooking lessons if you want," Abby offered, looking past Nate.

"Thanks, Abby," he said softly. "But I think we can all agree that there's no hope for me there."

I stood there for a few minutes, enjoying the banter as they all gave each other a hard time about who messed up what, taking the focus off of Jones. It wasn't a shock to anyone when he burned food, but we all still felt bad for him that he couldn't cook to save his life.

With Abby busy and distracted by Nate, I decided it was time to head to work.

"Alright, I gotta go. Talk later?" I said, leaning in to hug her.

"Sounds good. Let me know how it goes."

"It's just parent-teacher conferences," I laughed. "Nothing exciting is going to happen."

"Well, I wouldn't blame you if you decided to act out some naughty schoolgirl fantasy while you were there." She winked and wiggled her eyebrows.

"You're terrible," I called over my shoulder as I headed to the door and left.

The rest of the day was a complete blur. My brain wanted to focus on seeing Dominic, so no matter how hard I tried, I couldn't stop myself. I was counting down the hours like a silly little schoolgirl—not the kind Abby mentioned—desperate to see her crush. But, the problem was that even though I felt attracted to him, I knew nothing could happen between us.

By the time I got to the kid's school, my stomach was a giant ball of nerves, and my palms wouldn't stop sweating. Thankfully, Sally's conference was first, which gave me time to try to calm myself before I met with Dominic.

I sat there, listening the best I could, as her teacher sang her praises about what an outstanding student she was and how she was exceeding in a few subjects.

"I wanted to talk to you about moving Sally into a gifted class," Ms. Andrews said, folding her hands in front of her on the desk. "She's a bright girl, and I feel like she would do well if challenged more. I can tell she's easily getting bored in class as she's the first to complete the assignments and work on her homework when she's done. There's not much else that I can do for her, but if we put her into the gifted class, I think she would really excel."

I smiled proudly and knew that she was on the right path, as it was something I had been thinking about recently, too. Sally had always been one of those kids with a thirst for knowledge, and I made sure she had as many avenues to explore as possible.

"I think that's a wonderful idea," I agreed.

We talked about what the process would be from there, so I felt lighter and less stressed by the time I got to Dominic for Mikey's conference.

I was sitting in the chair in the hallway, right outside the classroom, waiting for Dominic to finish with the parent ahead of me. My foot tapped lightly on the linoleum floor until the door opened, and a couple walked out, beaming brightly as Dominic held the door open behind them.

"Ms. Hughes, come on in," he said, grinning his beautiful, dimpled grin. I got up, smiled, and kept my hands to myself to keep from reaching out and touching him.

I walked into the room and waited for him to join me when I heard another voice.

"Hold the door," Rick called, sticking his foot in to catch it before it closed.

I spun around, narrowing my eyes as if I couldn't believe he was there.

"Rick?" I questioned. "What are you doing here?"

He squeezed through the door, adjusting the jacket to his designer suit.

"I'm here for Mikey's parent-teacher conference."

I shook my head and pulled my eyebrows together.

"Why?"

"Because I'm his father, and I care about how he's doing at school," he bit out aggressively.

"Okay," I breathed in heavily and then forced it. "So, where were you for Sally's?"

"I got here as soon as I could, okay? You don't have to jump down my throat the second you see me, Jane."

The stress levels that had finally started to subside not that long ago were skyrocketing back up again.

"Why don't we get started?" Dominic asked, extending his hand to the desks across from his.

I sat down and felt my body stiffen the moment Rick sat next to me.

"Thank you both for coming today," Dominic said, looking between us. "While I haven't had the pleasure of being Mikey's teacher for the entire school year, I can say that I have truly enjoyed having him in class while I took over for Mrs. Crawford. Today, I'd like to begin with the notes she left regarding her time spent with him, and then we'll move into my observations and recommendations."

I nodded and tried to be pleasant, but Rick had this way of making my fangs come out.

Dominic went over the notes from Mrs. Crawford and then began talking to us about how Mikey was doing academically. I focused the best I could, but when he shifted gears to how he was doing socially, I wasn't prepared for what I was about to hear.

"Mikey is a very smart, very empathetic student who goes out of his way to help others," he started. "However, I've noticed recently that his demeanor seems to have shifted some, and I've witnessed a bit more aggression with him. It's been little things here and there, but I did have to step in and talk to him the other day after he threw his textbook on the floor. He was frustrated because he couldn't figure out the answer he was looking for."

"Okay," I said slowly. "I'll talk with him and see what's going on. Thank you for bringing this to my attention."

"No problem," he replied, then glanced at Rick, who was busy looking at something on his phone instead of paying attention. "My goal is to help all my students succeed, in and out of the classroom. I know that a lot of times there are things happening in their personal lives, and sometimes it helps to mention it during these conferences."

"I appreciate the insight."

I stood up and shook Dominic's hand, not bothering to acknowledge Rick as I walked out of the classroom and let the door close behind me.

A few minutes later, I heard loud footsteps coming down the hallway. I pulled my shoulders back and tried to take a few deep breaths before Rick got there.

"Jane, wait a minute," he called out. "We need to talk."

I stopped, folded my arms over my chest, and turned around. I didn't bother to fake a smile or pretend I was happy to see him—especially after the bullshit he pulled yesterday when the kids dropped the fish they caught off, and he couldn't care less.

"What do you want, Rick?"

He pulled his head back as if he was surprised that I was anything but thrilled to see him.

"What's going on between you and Mikey's teacher?"

"Excuse me?" I frowned and tilted my head.

"You heard me. Do you really think it's in your son's best interest to start dating his teacher?"

"What are you talking about?"

He rolled his eyes and then arched an eyebrow at me.

"Don't play stupid, Jane. Everyone in town has been talking about you two at the supermarket the other day."

I shook my head and sighed.

"You've got to be kidding me."

"I'm not. Mikey mentioned that he went fishing with you guys too."

"He did."

"Whatever this thing is between you two," he pointed from me to the door to Dominic's classroom. "It needs to stop. Now."

I pulled my head back and felt my blood starting to boil.

"First of all—nothing is going on between us. Second—it's none of your business if there was."

"It is when it involves my kids. He's too young for you, Jane. Have some standards."

"Really?" I shrieked, trying my best to keep my voice down. "That coming from you? The guy who is marrying a woman *twenty years* younger than him? The same guy who doesn't bother to be involved in his kids' lives to begin with. Get the fuck out of here with that bullshit, Rick. I don't have the time or the patience for this—hence why I divorced you in the first place."

"Wow, such a lady."

I rolled my eyes, making sure he saw it.

"Did you come today just so you could see if something was happening between Mikey's teacher and me?" I asked, suddenly seeing the pieces click into place. "Is that why you're here? Why you didn't even bother showing up for Sally's conference?"

"No," he lied. "I wanted to be there for both. It's not my fault that I got caught up at work and couldn't make it for hers."

"Okay, then why did you tell them yesterday that you couldn't make it? Seems like you didn't want to be bothered with it until you heard rumors about Dominic and me."

His eyebrows shot up on his forehead.

"Since when do you call their teachers by their first names?"

"You're reading too much into something that is none of your business. Now, if you'll excuse me, I need to get home to cook dinner for *my* kids."

I turned on my heel and stormed off, not bothering to respond to any of the insults he shot my way as I left.

Twelve
Dominic

The week wrapped up quickly, and I was thankful it was finally the weekend. Next week was spring break, but I still had plenty of work that I needed to get done and lesson plans to create. While I hoped to take some time off to spend with Olivia, my parents insisted on ensuring they still got their regularly scheduled "Olivia time."

Saturday morning, I'd woken up to a group text message, though the only numbers I had stored in my phone were from Nate and Jane. I assumed the other one was Abby's since there was a message from it with a picture of Penny and a kid's suitcase; the text stating *weekend sleepover at grandma and grandpa's house is a go!*

Jane replied, confirming that Sally and Mikey were staying over as well and that they were all having a movie night. I wasn't sure what to say, so I just sat there, watching the messages and laughing as they all picked on each other.

Nate: Since we have a kid-free night, what games are we playing? Poker?

Jane: It's my turn to host, and I don't have a poker table. Monopoly? Drunken Uno? Take your pick.

Unknown: I don't think any of us can handle drunken Uno.

Nate: We all know how that went last time anyway.

Unknown: It was a great excuse for Jane to buy a new coffee table. Never imagined she'd be such a sore loser.

Nate: I did. Apparently, it runs in the family.

Unknown: Shut your face, or you'll be on diaper-changing duty for the next month.

Jane: Pick your battles wisely, Nate.

Nate: Dominic—why aren't you saying anything?! Why are you letting these crazy ass women attack me like this?!

Unknown: You think this is being attacked?? You haven't seen anything yet.

Jane: Yeah, calm down. It's not like she's pregnant and has a plate of bacon.

Unknown: I can't eat that much bacon unless I'm knocked up. It makes me sick to my stomach these days.

Nate: Stop scaring Dominic off. He's on this message too, and you guys are going to make him rethink coming tonight.

Nate: Hey man, if you're there, type something. It's okay if you're scared. Just send an emoji or something to let me know you're okay. (wink face emoji)

I threw my head back and laughed before I replied.

Me: I'm not sure if I should be entertained or terrified. (scared face emoji)

Unknown: You went fishing with my sister. There

shouldn't be much that scares you at this point.

Nate: This is very true. I'm surprised you came back in one piece.

Jane: I'm NOT A BAD FISHER.

Unknown: You're not a good one. (shrugging emoji)

Me: She did really well!

Unknown: You're just saying that because you're afraid of her. It's okay, Dominic. This is a safe place. Tell us how you really feel.

Jane: Abby….

Nate: I heard that you also out fished her…

Me: Hey, I don't ever play to lose.

Nate: You were a brave soul, my man.

Unknown: Just when I was starting to like you and get to know you. (sad face emoji)

Jane: Hey, I caught some fish too! And if you all don't knock it off, I'm not feeding you dinner tonight.

Unknown: I can cook, so your threats are meaningless unless you were planning to pick up food from Surf 'N Shack—in that case, you're the world's best sister, and I love you more than anything in the world.

Jane: That's a lie, and you know it. There are a handful of things you love more than me.

Nate: But not Surf 'N Shack. (laughing emoji)

Jane: Anyways… Dominic, are you joining us tonight?

You're more than welcome to bring Olivia.

Nate: Nope—no kids tonight. I can find a sitter for you if needed.

Jane: Stop it, Nate!

Me: Not to worry, I'm sure my parents will jump at the opportunity to watch her. Jane, I would love to join you guys. What can I bring?

Unknown: (dots bouncing)

Unknown: (dots bouncing)

Jane: Ignore whatever comes from Abby. She's probably drunk.

Nate: Don't worry—I took her phone and stuck it down my pants.

Jane: Eew.

Nate: She'll be busy for a while trying to retrieve it. We'll see you guys tonight. Bringing a six-pack of beer and some hot wings.

Jane: Okay, I'll order a few pizzas.

Me: Want me to bring dessert?

Unknown: Oh, I'm sure you will. (wink face emoji)

Nate: I forget the phone in the pants trick only worked when we were "just friends". (face palm emoji)

Jane: Thank you, Dominic. Dessert would be fantastic.

I stared at the screen, waiting to see if there was more. I couldn't ignore the way I felt when I saw Abby's text and wondered if maybe Jane had been talking to her about me. Was it possible that Jane was feeling the same attraction to me that I felt for her?

Thirteen

Jane

I smoothed down the fabric of my denim skirt, trying to convince myself that I'd put it on because it was what I would wear to a typical adult-only game night with Abby and Nate and that I wasn't wearing it because Dominic was coming.

My parents had come by to pick the kids up an hour ago, and I'd taken the time to shower and get ready in peace. The pizza was already ordered, a few bottles of wine were chilling in the fridge, and a handful of games were set out on the coffee table for everyone to pick from when they got there.

The doorbell rang at six, startling me from my dirty daydream that I was lost in about Dominic coming through on his promise to bring dessert.

I opened the door and felt a rush of relief wash over me when Abby and Nate stood on the other side.

"Wow," Abby said, smirking as she leaned in for a hug. "I didn't get the memo that tonight was a dress-up kind of game night."

"Stop it," I hissed in her ear. "I just felt like wearing a skirt since the weather's nice," I lied.

"Okay, sure." She shrugged and hung her purse on the coat rack behind the door. "That makes total sense since we'll be inside, and you won't be able to enjoy it."

My face flushed with embarrassment, everything from my neck to my ears turning red.

"Leave her alone," Nate whispered loud enough for me to hear. "I'm sure she just wants to make it easier for Dominic to get his dessert."

"I hate you guys," I muttered, hugging Nate as the doorbell rang again. "You two better be on your best behavior tonight. I mean it." I pointed my finger at them and then opened the door.

"Hi," I said, my voice oddly high and filled with anxiety.

"Hey," he replied coolly.

"Come on in." I stepped back and made room for him to step inside.

"I wasn't sure what everyone liked, so I picked up an assorted cheesecake sampler."

I closed the door and smiled as he handed it to me.

"That was very thoughtful, thank you. This looks delicious." I took it into the kitchen and set it in the fridge.

The pizza had come a few minutes after everyone got there, which was the perfect distraction from the way Dominic's eyes kept wandering over my legs.

We all sat at the kitchen table, Nate and Abby on one side, Dominic and me on the other. It felt very much like we were on a double date, and the jolts of electricity I felt every time his leg "accidentally" brushed against mine made me wish we were.

"This pizza is so good," Abby said around a mouthful.

"It's a sin," Nate commented, making a grossed-out face.

"No, it is not!"

I laughed and turned toward Dominic.

"Alright, where do you stand on the issue—are you team pineapple on pizza or team no pineapple?"

He looked between Abby and Nate, working his jaw back and forth as he thought about his answer.

"Ummm. Team no pineapple, I guess." He shrugged and earned a wink from Nate.

"That's right, my man. Pineapple doesn't belong on pizza," Nate said.

"I don't get what the big deal is," Abby whined, taking another bite of her slice.

"It's gross." Nate scrunched his nose at her.

"No, it's not. You're gross."

"Real mature comeback there, Mrs. Wilson."

"Hey, I take my pineapple very seriously," she replied, picking a piece off and offering it between her fingers to Nate.

"Nope, I don't want it."

"Why not? You like pineapple."

"Not after it's been on pizza!"

I laughed and shook my head.

"Alright, why are you team no pineapple? Is it no pineapple

in general, or just not on pizza?" I asked Dominic.

"Honestly," he leaned in and whispered quietly. "I have no problem with pineapple on pizza, but don't tell *them* that. I'm still trying to stay on Nate's good side. But in general, there are plenty of other places that I'd rather eat it from."

His eyes trailed from mine down to my chest and then to my skirt, which suddenly felt too tight.

He lifted his slice and took a bite, licking his lips as he watched me.

My body suddenly felt on fire, and I wanted nothing more than for Dominic to put it out and show me what else that tongue of his could do.

We finished eating and cleared off the table while the guys decided which game we would play first. Since Abby and I were the most competitive, we agreed that letting them choose what we beat them in would only be fair.

I wiped down the kitchen table and opened a bottle of wine while everyone got situated.

Nate chose Monopoly, but Abby quickly vetoed it after the last time we played, and she threatened to divorce him if he took another one of her hotels. Dominic suggested Scrabble, and I was surprised they were quick to jump on board since it wasn't a game we usually played.

We sat spread out on all four sides of the table so no one could cheat and see our letter tiles. Since Dominic was new to our game nights, we agreed that he should go first. I wasn't surprised when he jumped out of the gate with a high-point value word with *zombie*.

Nate grumbled about how it wasn't fair to play with someone who was a teacher, but Abby nudged him and told him to stop being a sourpuss, or she wouldn't put out later.

We laughed and gave each other shit about making up fake words while we enjoyed an adult night without kids. It wasn't often that I got to have these, but I was thankful for it tonight. Maybe it was just because Dominic was there, but it felt different. I felt more liberated—and not just because of the three glasses of wine I'd had. Perhaps it was because I had gotten myself ready for this one and put effort into looking nice, but deep down, I couldn't get past the way I felt every time Dominic looked at me like I was some prize that he wanted to win.

He sparked a fire deep inside, and I was ready for more.

The night wound down, and by nine o'clock, Abby and Nate were pretending they were tired when we all knew that they just wanted to get home and jump each other's bones—Nate's words, not mine. Dominic offered to stick around for a few and help me clean up, which shot my nerves through the roof when I imagined being alone with him.

"Drive safely. Let me know when you get home," I called to Nate and Abby as they climbed into his truck and took off.

I closed the door and slowly pulled a deep breath in, holding it in my lungs for a few seconds as I tried to steady my nerves. I could hear Dominic in the kitchen, so I headed in and found him at the sink, washing dishes.

"You don't have to do that," I said softly, folding my arms over my chest as I leaned against the doorframe, shamelessly taking in the sight in front of me.

"I don't mind. But I also don't want to overstay my welcome, so feel free to kick me out anytime you want."

I swallowed hard and dropped my hands, rubbing them along the front of my skirt.

"What time do you need to pick Olivia up?" I asked, my voice shaky.

He turned off the water, grabbed the towel to dry his hands, and then turned to look at me.

"My parents are keeping her overnight."

"Oh," I stammered. "Um, would you like another beer?"

I walked to the fridge and opened it, my hand reaching out to grab one when he came up behind me and covered it with his own.

"I'd rather not but thank you."

His words vibrated against my ear, the deep timbre sending goosebumps across my skin.

"Would you like something else instead?"

"A glass of water would be great."

"Okay. I'll get it."

When I turned around, he was right there, invading my space and pinning me in the small area between the fridge and his body. He took a step back, allowing me to move, but something came over me instead.

Without giving it much thought, I leaped into his arms, latched onto his neck, and wrapped my legs around his waist like some sort of crazed spider monkey.

It was crazy—insane—and not something I would ever think of doing, but right then, at the moment, I wasn't thinking. I was acting on impulse, going after the one thing I wanted more than anything—him.

His hands quickly grabbed my ass and held me in place as he pushed me against the freezer door. I lowered my mouth to his, my tongue gently sliding across his lips as it begged for access. A growl escaped his throat as he kissed me, one hand lifting to cup my face while the other stayed planted firmly on my backside.

I pulled away briefly to catch my breath, letting my head fall to the side as he hungrily kissed down the side of my neck. I whimpered, feeling the ache between my thighs as my body responded so quickly to him.

His tongue slid across my collarbone and then moved up to the other side of my neck, kissing and nipping along the way up to my ear.

I was panting as I arched my back and tried to push my hips up to get some friction rubbing against his jeans. While I had thought long and hard about all of the reasons why this *shouldn't* happen, none of that mattered right now. There was nothing I wanted more than for this *to* happen, but that didn't completely silence the thoughts in my head. It was like my body and my mind were in two different places, each begging for something different.

"We shouldn't be doing this," I moaned, my fingers grabbing the short locks of hair that were trimmed right above his neck. "You're too young for me."

"I'm not that young," he countered as his mouth moved down my neck again.

I rocked my hips against him, pulling him closer with my legs.

"Fuck, Jane," he breathed out. "You're making it really hard to control myself right now."

I let my head fall back against the freezer and closed my eyes.

"I like it hard."

I didn't have time to regret what I'd said because his hand slipped off of my ass and slid around to my exposed thigh as he pressed his erection into me while holding me in place.

"Is this hard enough?"

"Let's go to my room," I panted, my thighs shaking around him.

Slowly he helped me to my feet, then took my hand as I rushed us to it.

I closed the door and stood in front of him, locking eyes as I lifted the bottom of his shirt and pulled it over his head. My fingers grazed along the tight muscles that outlined his abs, trailing up to his chiseled chest. He looked like one of those guys you'd slap on the front of a steamy romance book cover that all of the women would go crazy for.

He lifted his hand and gently brushed his finger over my lip.

"You have such big hands," I said, closing my eyes as I soaked up his touch.

"All the better to touch you with." He leaned in, pressed his lips to my temple, and then softly kissed his way down to my lips.

"Such soft lips," I murmured.

"All the better to kiss you with."

My hands wandered freely over his defined body, enjoying every bit of it.

"Such a muscular body," I practically panted as his hands reached down and grabbed my ass.

"All the better to please you with."

"Are you talking dirty to me in Little Red Riding Hood style?"

His chuckle vibrated against my skin before he pulled his head back and looked at me.

"Maybe. What can I say? I read a lot of nursery rhymes."

My cheeks split into a goofy grin and I knew at that moment that I was a goner.

"You didn't compliment my teeth," he said coyly, pulling my body closer to his.

"Well, you do have a great smile. Perfectly straight teeth. White. Very impressive."

He laughed and scrubbed a hand down his face.

"Thank you," he said, still smiling. "I appreciate the compliment but didn't see it going that direction in my head."

"What direction was it supposed to go?" I tilted my head and studied his beautiful face.

"You were supposed to say *my, what big teeth you have.* And then I was going to say, all the better to eat you with."

Something changed in his eyes and I felt the arousal

pooling between my thighs.

"Oh," I whispered. "Well, they are quite big now that you mention it."

He arched an eyebrow and slowly ran his hands up my sides, lifting my shirt in the process.

"I guess that means it's time to eat."

Fourteen

Dominic

Jane stood before me in just her bra and the little denim skirt that had been tormenting me all night. It was short enough to make me curious to know what she had on underneath it but not too short to make her look inappropriate.

"Would you like that?" I asked, brushing a strand of hair out of her face. "Do you want me to eat you?"

Her chest rose and fell heavily as she nodded her head yes.

I lowered my head and kissed her lips, gently pushing her back to the bed. As soon as we reached it, I lifted her waist and gently lowered her down in the middle.

I licked my lips and then hovered over her as I unbuttoned her skirt before pulling it down her legs and tossing it to the floor. A black lace thong greeted me, matching the bra that needed to come off next. But for now, I wanted to be between her legs and wasn't going to waste any time.

She studied me, her eyes watching my every move as I lowered myself and started planting kisses along her stomach. Suddenly, she flinched, and I felt her hands pushing my head away. At first, I thought she was just desperate for me to go down on her, but then I realized that it wasn't desire that was making her act this way. It was fear.

I pulled back and looked up at her, catching the look in her eye.

"What's wrong? Do you want me to stop?"

She shook her head and looked away.

"Jane," I said gently. "Please talk to me. Tell me what happened. We don't have to do anything you don't want to."

"It's not that," she assured me.

"Okay, then what happened?"

"Nothing," she lied, refusing to look me in the eye.

"Jane, please."

She sighed heavily and lifted her hand to cover her face.

"I just don't want you to see my body."

I pulled my head back in confusion. Why wouldn't she want me to see her body? It was gorgeous and I couldn't wait to taste every inch of it.

"Jane, you're beautiful. Every single part of you. You have nothing to hide from me."

She laughed, but it sounded strained.

"Yes I do."

"Like what?"

"Stretch marks. A c-section scar. Flab that never went away after having Sally. I'm not young and tight like women your age, Dominic. I'm an old lady with an old lady body."

I covered my mouth with my fist and tried to hide the laugh.

"That's not true. You're not old, Jane."

"Yes, I am. You're just being nice."

I could still hear the hesitancy in her voice and decided to do something about it.

"Do you trust me?" I asked, lying down beside her.

She looked over at me, and I made sure that my eyes stayed focused on hers and not anywhere else on her body.

"I know you have things you're insecure about. We all have them. But if you give me a chance, I can show you what I see when I look at you."

She pulled her lower lip between her teeth and chewed it nervously.

"How are you going to do that?"

"You'll see. But you have to trust me, okay? And Jane, if there's anything that makes you uncomfortable and you want me to stop, I need you to say so. Okay?"

I could see her debating whether to allow herself to do this, but then she gave in and nodded.

I climbed off of the bed and then reached my hand out to her. She sat up, allowing me to guide her until she was sitting on the side, her butt right on the edge. There was a full-length mirror on the wall across from us, so I lined her up so she would be able to see herself in it.

Then I lowered myself to the floor, spreading her legs in front of me as I slowly leaned in and kissed her thigh.

"I want you to watch me eat you out in the mirror, Jane," I said as I licked up one side and down the other. "I want you to see how fucking turned on I am right now and how much your body sends me over the edge. I want you to watch my tongue as it teases your clit and brings you to the best orgasm you've ever had. I want you to see how beautiful you look when you're coming, how amazing your body is."

Before she could object, I started pulling her panties down and pinned her with a look until she lifted her hips so I could take them off.

"Good girl," I whispered before tossing them to the floor.

I locked eyes with her as I grabbed her hips and tugged her closer to the edge of the bed without letting her fall.

"Watch me eat you, Jane. Keep your eyes on the mirror, and then tell me this isn't the most amazing thing you've ever seen."

Her pupils were dilated, but she didn't argue as she looked past me to the mirror that was only a few feet away from us.

I lowered my head, nudging her thighs to open further, making sure she could see everything. I angled my body so she could watch my tongue as I licked her lips, gently teasing her clit with a few flicks.

She moaned, urging me to keep going.

I kissed her clit before pulling it in and sucking, loving the way her nails suddenly dug into my shoulders. I teased her for a few more seconds before going back to licking her, her desperate cries a beautiful song to my ears.

"Watch yourself in the mirror," I coaxed. "See how wet you are for me?"

Her hips moved as she tried to push herself closer to my face.

"Such an eager girl," I laughed. "Don't worry, I'm going to eat this pussy the way you want. I'm going to make you come so hard you see stars. Then I'm going to fuck you so good that you won't want anyone's dick but mine."

I felt her thighs tremble against my head as her nails scratched down my neck.

"Yes," she cried softly. "Yes, Dominic. I want all of that."

"I'm going to give it to you, baby. Keep your eyes on that mirror."

I regained my focus, positioning my head between her thighs as I tortured her with my tongue. I looked up as she came, satisfied when I saw her eyes locked on the mirror like I'd asked. Within seconds, her pussy spasmed around my tongue as I sucked harder, licking up every single drop of arousal.

Once she was done, I slowly pulled away and sat back on my heels. I chewed my lower lip, looking at the satisfaction on her face.

"You ready for more?" I asked.

She nodded and ran a hand across my cheek tenderly.

"That was amazing," she said.

"You haven't seen anything yet."

I got up, lifted her, and then tossed her over my shoulder as she squealed.

"Dominic! What are you doing?" she laughed.

I opened the bedroom door and carried her down the

hallway and into the kitchen, where I grabbed one of the chairs. I shifted her weight on my shoulder and then balanced the chair on my other arm as I took her back to the bedroom.

"You really are strong, aren't you?" she asked, still smiling as she lifted her head and looked over her shoulder to see what I was doing.

"You know it."

I set the chair down in front of the mirror, then used my free hand to slap her bare ass. She yelped, but the look in her eyes said that it turned her on as much as it did me.

"What are you doing with the chair?" she asked as I quickly fished a condom out of my wallet before tossing my jeans to the floor.

I held the foil packet between my teeth as I hooked my thumbs into the top of my briefs and pulled them down.

She didn't wait for my answer as her eyes trailed down and landed on my dick as it sprung free. It was hard and begging for a release.

"We're not done with the mirror," I said, nodding to it as I stroked myself, her eyes still locked on it.

"We're not?" she asked but didn't bother to look up.

"Nope."

I stepped forward and grabbed her hand, replacing it with mine. She eagerly took over stroking me as I closed my eyes and tried not to come.

"Alright, let's go," I said abruptly a few minutes later. "I don't want to come in your hand."

"Okay," she giggled, letting go.

"Are you still sure you want this?" I asked, making sure we were both still on the same page.

"Mm hmm." She wasn't looking at me, just focused on my cock.

I pinched her chin between my finger and thumb and guided her head up slightly until she looked at me.

"I'm glad he impresses you, but I have even more to show you."

"Okay."

I took her hand and led her to the chair in front of the mirror.

"What are we doing with that?"

I tore open the foil and sheathed myself before tossing the empty package on the dresser.

"I'm going to sit down, and you're going to ride me."

She opened her mouth to object but then snapped it shut.

"We're both going to watch in the mirror," I added. "It's going to be so fucking hot to watch my dick slide in and out of you, Jane."

I sat down on the chair, thankful that it didn't have arms so we didn't have to worry about it being too tight of a space. I leaned back against the tall back and finger motioned her to join me.

She tried covering her body with her hands before attempting to mount me with her back to the mirror.

"Nope," I said quickly, holding my hand up to stop her. "Turn around, baby."

She sighed heavily but did as I asked.

Once she was lined up, I held my cock in one hand and caressed her thigh with the other as she slid down on top of me.

I closed my eyes and held my breath as I got used to the sensation. It felt beyond incredible the way she wrapped so tightly around me.

"Ahhh," she cried out and sank lower until I was fully seated inside her.

I moved my hands up and unhooked her bra before flinging it across the room. Then I slid them around her stomach and pulled her close to me, so her back rested against my chest while we both adjusted to me being inside her.

"You're so fucking beautiful," I whispered, catching her eye in the mirror. "So beautiful, Jane."

I caressed her breasts and kissed her neck as I rocked my hips and felt her match my rhythm as she started to ride me. Her feet were tucked behind my legs, so I spread them further, forcing her legs to spread wider.

"Do you see that?" I asked, nodding to the mirror. "Do you see me sliding inside of you? Do you like watching your pussy as my cock thrusts in and out of it? You're so fucking tight."

We were closer to the mirror than she was when I went down on her, and the way I had her body held against mine gave us the perfect view as we fucked.

I lifted my hips quickly, fucking her the best I could in this position while she watched. Then, when I knew she was already turned on and into it, I lowered my hands from her breasts and slid them along her stomach, caressing the stretch marks and c-section scar she was so worried about.

At first, she started to flinch, but I held her in place and shook my head.

"Do you feel how hard I just got, Jane? That's how much you turn me on. Your body is perfect. Never doubt that."

I thrust harder, trying not to close my eyes as she ground down and rotated her hips. I could feel her squeezing me, teasing me to the breaking point.

My fingers dipped lower, rubbing her clit, forcing her to moan louder as she came closer to another orgasm.

"Come with me, baby," I coaxed. "Now, Jane, come now!"

She cried out with pleasure as I felt her pussy spasm against my fingers and cock. I grunted as I filled the condom with my load, my toes curled with how intense it was.

We sat there for a few minutes, breathing heavily as she lay against me, her body completely relaxed.

I didn't want to rush the moment—hell, I didn't want to ever leave this position with Jane—but I needed to get up and deal with the condom. I kissed her temple and ran my fingers up and down her arms.

"That was amazing," she said lazily.

"You're amazing, so obviously the sex would be too," I replied with a goofy smile plastered on my face.

"Are you hungry? There's still some pizza left over," she offered, looking back at me.

"Sure. Sounds great. I'll go clean up real quick and meet you in the kitchen."

"Okay."

She climbed off of me slowly while I held the condom in place. I grabbed the foil packet from the dresser while she slipped into the walk-in closet and pulled out a long t-shirt that she pulled over her head.

"I'll meet you in there."

I smiled and then headed to the guest bathroom across the hall. I didn't want the kids to find the condom or the wrapper accidentally, so I grabbed some tissue to dispose of it but stopped suddenly when I noticed my hand was wet. I looked down, finding a small tear in the bottom.

"Fuck," I muttered, slamming my hand down on the counter.

I grabbed the wad of tissue and finished disposing of it, then cleaned up and got dressed. When I walked into the kitchen, Jane was standing at the microwave, warming up pizza as the shirt she was wearing rode up high enough for me to see her bare ass.

I opened the trash can and tossed everything inside, dreading having to tell her what had just happened.

"Hey, you. Do you want sausage, pepperoni, or the ham/ pineapple combo?" she asked cheerfully, her face quickly falling when she noticed the change in my demeanor.

"Are you suddenly team no pineapple? Because there's plenty of the other ones left." She pointed to the boxes sitting on the counter. "I always order extra so I have a quick lunch for the kids, but they like pineapple too, so it's no big dea—"

I stood in front of her and lifted my finger to her lips.

"The pizza is fine, thank you."

Her shoulder relaxed slightly, but I could tell she still sensed something was off.

"Okay," she breathed out. "What's wrong?"

I ran a hand through my hair and pressed my lips together.

"The condom broke."

Fifteen
Jane

"What do you mean it broke?" I stared at him in disbelief while the microwave continued to ding behind me.

"I went to dispose of it and noticed that some was leaking out of the tip. When I checked, there was a small tear. I'm sorry, Jane."

My mind was racing a mile a minute as I tried to figure out what to do.

"It's not your fault. These things happen," I said shakily.

It wasn't like I didn't know what to do if something like this happened, but now that it was happening to me, I was drawing a complete blank.

"Do you want to sit down? You look a little pale." Dominic extended his hand to me, but I couldn't get my body to move to take it.

I blinked a couple of times, trying to clear the fog with no luck.

"Jane?"

"Hmmm?"

I turned my head to look at him but still couldn't focus.

"Are you okay? I know this wasn't what either of us expected, and I promise you I'm clean. I can schedule an appointment this week to get tested if you'd like to see the results for yourself. I get tested every year with my annual physical."

I let out a shaky breath, my legs suddenly feeling wobbly.

As if already being completely in tune with my body, Dominic wrapped an arm around my waist and led me to the table. I looked at the chairs and noticed the spot where one was missing. The one we just had sex on when the condom broke. *When did it break? How much had he come inside of me? Did it break when he tried to take it off? Did it break before we even started?*

I sat down but couldn't get my thoughts to go to anything other than the stupid condom.

Dominic went to the microwave, pulled out one plate, and popped in the other before starting it. Then he came over, set a bottle of water on the table in front of me, and sat beside me.

"I'm really sorry, Jane. This has never happened to me; honestly, I don't even know how it happened."

I lifted the bottle and took a sip. Then another. I kept going until I'd downed more than half of it and had to stop to catch my breath. I wiped my mouth with the back of my hand and set it back on the table.

"I'm on the pill," I blurted out.

He leaned back in his chair and ran a hand down the stubble on his jaw.

"Okay, good. That's good."

I nodded, hating the sting of disappointment that suddenly

decided to bubble up inside me.

He was glad that I was on the pill. Did that he mean that he didn't want any more children? Did this mean that I secretly wanted to have children with him, and that's why I felt disappointed with his reaction? What was I hoping he'd say—bummer, I was really hoping you weren't on anything, so my super sperm could rip open the condom and knock you up!

I shook my head, embarrassed by the thoughts, and focused on the microwave that was beeping again.

"Your pineapple-covered pizza is ready," I joked, hoping to change the subject for the time being.

He got up and grabbed it, then joined me at the table with the other plate as well.

We ate in silence for a few minutes, both of us lost in our own worlds as we processed what had just happened.

The problem was that I didn't want to focus on the broken condom part. I wanted to go back and relive the super-hot sex part. While I was beyond nervous about trusting him, I was glad that I did because he was right—it was fucking sexy to watch as he ate me out, but even hotter to see him inside of me.

But all of that was short-lived because, at the end of the day, we still had other problems to worry about besides the condom breaking.

<u>Sixteen</u>
Dominic

It had been a whole week since I'd talked to Jane. After that night, she basically ghosted me whenever I reached out to her. Every time I invited her to join Olivia and me for dinner, she had an excuse as to why she couldn't make it. By Saturday, she'd even skipped the weekly pizza dinner at Abby and Nate's house when she found out I'd been invited.

I would have gladly stayed home and skipped it so she could go, but Nate told me not to worry about it. While he and Abby didn't know that we'd slept together—or at least I didn't think they knew—they could tell something was going on with her.

The kids were still camping with their grandparents until Sunday, so she claimed she needed to get things ready at home before they got back. I knew she was avoiding me, but I didn't know why.

By Tuesday, I'd taken time to get in with a doctor, so I could have the results to put her mind at ease. When I'd asked her to join me for coffee so I could show her, she claimed she was good and too busy with work to get away for a few.

Monday morning came quickly, and I found myself studying Mikey for any indication of how his mom was doing. It wasn't like I could just come out and ask him without sounding weird. Plus, I didn't want to embarrass him in front of the other kids.

So, I'd gone about the day, getting the class on track and trying to keep Jane out of my head. By lunchtime, I'd sat at my desk, poking at my sandwich with no desire to eat it. There was a commotion outside by the window, with kids yelling and a few screaming for someone to stop. I jumped up and ran outside, turning to find Mikey fighting another kid.

I quickly grabbed him while another teacher pulled the other student away. They instantly tried going for each other again, so I nodded at the other teacher, then pulled Mikey into my classroom and shut the door.

His face was red, and there was a mark on his head that was raised and swollen. I picked up the phone in my classroom, called the front desk to let them know what had happened and that I would be sending a student to the nurse's office.

"Do you want to tell me what that was all about?" I asked, folding my arms over my chest as I studied him.

His jaw was clenched as tight as his fists, anger still prominent on his face.

"Nothing."

"Obviously it was something, or you two wouldn't have gotten into a fight," I said softly.

"He's just a stupid bully," he muttered, looking at the floor.

I sat on the edge of my desk, keeping my posture as relaxed as possible.

"Is he bullying you?"

He shook his head, still refusing to meet my eyes.

"Who is he bullying?"

There was a knock on the door that led to the hallway. I waited for him to answer as one of the receptionists from the front desk came in and stood by the door, ready to escort him to the nurse's office. He'd likely be visiting the principal right after, but I wanted them to check the bump on his head first.

"No one."

"Mikey, I can't help you if you don't tell me. If he's bullying someone, I need to know so I can put a stop to it."

He looked from the receptionist to me and then back to her again.

"Sally."

I swallowed hard as I watched him walk across the room and go with her to the nurse's office.

There were only a few minutes left of lunch, but I knew I needed to call Jane and let her know what was happening.

I waited for her voicemail to pick up, knowing she wouldn't answer since she was at work, but also because it was me. I cleared my throat and then began as soon as her greeting ended.

"Hey, Jane. It's Dominic. There's been an incident at school, and Mikey was involved in a fight. He's okay, but I asked them to have the nurse check out the bump on his head. There's more that we need to talk about, so please call me back or stop by my classroom when you come to pick up Mikey. Thanks."

I hung up right as the bell rang. I shoved my phone into my pocket, hoping I would feel it when she called back—if she called back, then tossed my lunch in the trash and prepared for another round of rowdy kids.

By two thirty, I still hadn't heard anything from Jane. The front office confirmed that Mikey was still waiting to be picked up, so I was hoping I would be able to see Jane when she got there. School was ending in a few minutes, which would mean she could come talk to me.

I helped the kids finish cleaning up their supplies, and then the bell rang, dismissing them. I sat down at my desk and entered the last few notes I needed for the day when I heard a knock on the door.

I stood up, my heart racing as I hoped it was Jane on the other side.

"Come in," I called loudly, shoving my hands in my pockets as I sat on the edge of my desk and tried to act casual.

The door opened, and Jane stepped inside with Mikey and Sally in front of her.

"Go have a seat while I talk to Mr. Rosario," she instructed, pointing to a table in the back of the room. She looked tired, and I wondered if she had had a rough day.

"Sorry, I tried to get here sooner, but there was an emergency at work."

"Don't apologize," I said, holding my hands up. "It's not a problem. I hope everything is okay with whatever happened."

"Thank you. It was a bit chaotic, but everything is fine now. At work, anyway." She looked over to the table where the kids sat and shook her head.

"I'm sure you've heard about the fight," I said, keeping my voice low.

"I did. Though I have yet to hear what it was about."

I glanced at Mikey, noticing that the bump had decreased considerably, but now he was starting to sport a black eye.

"I don't have many details, but Mikey did confess that the other child he got into the fight with has been bullying Sally. I don't know what started the fight, but I could tell he was pretty upset about it."

"Sally?" She folded her arms over her chest, pressing the silk fabric between her breasts—not that I was staring at them.

I nodded.

"Neither of them has said anything to me about it. I can't believe they wouldn't tell me."

"Kids are like that sometimes, especially as they get older. Mikey probably thought he was doing the right thing by protecting his little sister."

She seemed to consider that for a moment as we watched them sit at the table and whisper between them.

"You guys, come here, please," she said sternly.

They both got up and walked over, standing in front of us.

"I want to know what happened today, Mikey. Why did you get in a fight?"

"It's not a big deal, mom."

She arched an eyebrow and gave him a look I never wanted to be on the receiving end of.

"Try again."

He puffed out a frustrated breath and shifted his weight.

"The kid was talking crap about Sally, and I didn't like it."

"So, you started a fight?"

"No."

"Okay, then, who started it?"

"He did."

"How?"

"By saying that she was a big baby because she still played with Barbies," Mikey said, raising his voice.

"And that started the fight?" Jane asked, keeping the dialogue between them flowing.

"No."

"Okay, then what did? You need to tell me everything that happened."

"Then, he said that I was a girl because I played with Barbies too."

I leaned against the desk and listened, hating how cruel kids could be to each other.

"And what did you do?"

"I told him he was stupid," Mikey muttered under his breath.

"Then what happened?"

"He swung at my head."

"Is that how you got the bump?" she asked, pointing to it.

"No, I ducked, and he fell to the ground. I tried to walk away, but he got up and hit me from behind. I turned around and started swinging. He hit me a few times. I hit him. Then Mr. Rosario came and pulled me away."

Jane pressed her mouth into a thin line and then looked at Sally.

"Sally, has this boy been bothering you too?"

She nodded and pulled at the straps of her backpack nervously.

"Why haven't either of you said anything?" Jane looked between them, her face softening. "I can't help you guys with these things if I don't know about it."

"I had it handled," Mikey said.

"Handled? You had it handled?" Her voice rose as high as her eyebrows. "Calling people names and fighting is not handling it, Mikey. That's the cowardly way of dealing with it."

"You could have come to me as well," I offered softly, catching Mikey's eye. "Not to say that you shouldn't tell your mom, but if you felt like you couldn't, then you should have come to me so I could take care of it. We don't allow bullying at school, but we can't do anything about it if we don't know it's happening. Our goal is to keep everyone safe. That's our job."

"I'm sorry," Mikey said, more irritated than sincere.

"Not to worry, you'll have plenty of time to think about stuff this week since you've been suspended. You can start with how to properly apologize to me and Mr. Rosario for the sarcastic one you just gave. Then you can think about how to handle things like this in the future."

"Fine," he added.

I didn't know if he had some sort of death wish, but I couldn't imagine things were going to go well for him talking to his mother that way.

"I need to talk to Mr. Rosario alone for a few minutes. You two can start your punishment by picking up trash in the hallway. We saw a few pieces on our way in. Go clean them up and wait by the door for me."

She stood there, waiting for them to do as she said.

Once the door shut and we were alone, she finally exhaled heavily, her chest rising and falling.

"I'm sorry about his attitude. He's not usually like this, and even though I talked to him after our parent-teacher conference, I haven't been able to get to the root of what the problem is."

"Don't worry about it. I get treated worse daily. Part of the job," I joked with a wink.

"He's usually such a nice kid with far less attitude."

"He's still a nice kid, and I can guarantee that the attitude is only going to get worse as he goes through puberty. But I do think there's something going on that's been bothering him. Has he mentioned anything about his dad?"

"No," she shook her head. "But then again, Rick has been distant with them since he got engaged. He didn't even check in with the kids when they got back from camping yesterday. My mom said they had a great time, and the kids seemed to have fun. I don't know what changed since then, but I need to get a handle on it before it escalates. I'm going to sit down with them tonight and talk about things that are changing with their dad to see if that's part of the problem. Now that I know about the bullying, we can deal with that too."

"I think that's a great place to start," I agreed, folding my hands in my lap.

"Thanks. Sorry for keeping you after school. We'll go and get out of your hair."

She turned to leave, but I grabbed her arm and stopped her before she could.

"Jane, I know you're avoiding me, and I would really appreciate it if you would talk to me and let me know why."

She froze in place, her body rigid with tension.

"Come on, one of us had to mention the elephant in the room. I've been calling and texting you for a week, and you've blown me off every chance you've had."

"I have not," she said defensively, turning to face me. "I've just been busy."

I pinned her with a look that called her on the lie, then watched her fidget with the sleeves of her blouse.

"Really? Because it feels like you're purposely ghosting me. I mean, I get it. If you just wanted to use me for my body, you could've just said so."

I chewed my lower lip as I watched her blush, a faint grin spreading across her face.

"That's not what I was doing," she hissed quietly, as if

embarrassed that someone might hear her.

"Then what are you doing? Because all I know is we had a really good time, and I sure as hell felt a connection between us, Jane. There was no faking the chemistry. I know that things got a little nerve-wracking with the condom breaking, but I assumed we would be able to talk about it like adults and deal with it. And not that you asked, but I have the results from my recent test, showing that I'm clean." I walked around my desk and pulled open the bottom drawer to retrieve the envelope.

I handed it to her, but she refused to take it.

"You didn't have to go get tested, Dominic."

"If it meant that you would talk to me, yeah, I did. It's been driving me crazy, Jane. I don't know what I did wrong, but I would really love the opportunity to fix it."

She sat down at one of the desks across from mine and held her head in her hands.

"You freaked me out," she admitted, looking up at me.

"I don't think I've heard that one before," I laughed. "But I'm sorry, I think?"

She rolled her eyes, realizing how silly she sounded.

"You freaked me out because I started to like you, and I had been telling myself all of the reasons why I couldn't."

"Which are?"

"I feel like there are too many to list," she laughed.

"Am I that bad?" I countered with a shocked expression.

"No, not at all. But Dominic, I'm ten years older than you.

I'm a single mom with an ex-husband who can be a prick 99% of the time. I love my job, but I don't know if it's a conflict of interest that I'm your daughter's pediatrician. And you're my son's teacher. He's already having a hard time with getting bullied at school—Sally too—the last thing that I want is to add to that by dating his teacher."

"Okay, fair enough. But your age doesn't bother me. I couldn't honestly care less. And I'll match your prick of an ex-husband with a drug addict ex-wife who walked out on us the day she had Olivia because she was so desperate to get high that she couldn't be bothered with her baby. She stayed clean the entire pregnancy, then went right back to the streets looking for her next fix the moment the hospital cleared her to leave. We all have our own baggage, Jane. It comes with being a single parent. I don't see any problem with you being Olivia's doctor, but if it bothers you, I'll find someone else. And I understand what you're saying about Mikey and Sally, I do. But Jane, kids are always going to find a reason to make fun of other kids. Are you really willing to hold yourself back from something *you* want just because they *might* get teased about it? I'm not disregarding your feelings, but I think you need to stop worrying about what everyone else wants and think about what it is you want."

"It's not that easy," she said sadly.

"It can be, but you have to be willing to try."

"I better get out there and check on them."

I nodded, knowing she was blowing me off again. I tried not to let my emotions show, but it was hard because I liked her so much and really wanted a chance to try to make this work.

She headed toward the door, adjusted her purse on her shoulder, then turned and looked at me.

"I'm making grilled cheese and tomato soup for dinner tonight if you and Olivia would like to join us."

"We'd love to," I answered with a grin that pulled my cheeks tightly across my face.

Seventeen

Jane

"Keep stirring the soup," I told Sally, keeping an eye to make sure that it didn't start boiling up and burn her. She loved to help in the kitchen, and I loved teaching her how to cook. Mikey was busy cleaning the kitchen table before setting it, part of his usual chores that he helped with because he didn't enjoy cooking.

After five, Dominic messaged me to tell me that they were on their way. A few minutes later, I heard the doorbell. I turned the stove off, moving the pot with the tomato soup to the trivet.

"Thank you, sweetie. Go wash up; we'll eat soon." I kissed Sally's head and guided her away from the stove as I headed to the door.

"Hey," I greeted, moving to the side so they could come in.

Olivia smiled brightly, reaching for me the way she did every time she saw me. I smiled and looked at Dominic before holding my hands out to take her.

"I think you're her new favorite person," he laughed, handing her to me. "I hope you don't mind, but I brought a veggie tray. I had too much at home and didn't want them to go bad."

"Of course not, thank you."

He headed to the kitchen as I followed behind, with Olivia snuggled close to my chest.

"Hey, Mikey," Dominic said, nodding to him as he set the plate down on the island.

"Hi."

I gave Mikey a look and then mouthed *sorry* to Dominic. Mikey had been in a sour mood since we got home, and it made me reconsider whether inviting Dominic and Olivia over for dinner was a good idea. While I knew I needed to sit down and talk to Mikey, I also felt terrible about making Dominic feel the way he had and didn't want to keep shutting him out.

I could invite him over and keep things at a *friend* level. I didn't have to jump his bones every time we were around each other. Plus, it would be different this time with the kids being here. We could just go back to the way things were before they got out of hand last Saturday. It was totally and completely doable.

"The sandwiches will be ready soon," I said, heading to the fridge to grab the ingredients. "I like to make mine a ham and cheese grilled cheese, but the kids prefer just cheese. Let me know what you guys would like, and I'll get them going."

"I'll do ham and cheese with you," he replied warmly as I handed Olivia back to him. I realized it was more complicated than I thought to get things out of the fridge with a curious infant attached to my hip.

"What about little miss Olivia?"

"She'll do plain cheese."

"Sounds great."

I set everything out by the stove, began buttering slices of bread, and then placed them face down in the skillet I'd turned on.

"Do you need any help?" Dominic offered.

"I'm good, but thank you. Mikey, when you're done wiping down the table, please set it with bowls for the soup."

"Yes, Mother."

I pressed my lips together to keep from scolding him for his attitude. I knew that it wouldn't do any good right now and would just further escalate things. I would rather wait until he was in a better mood and then discuss it.

I lined all of the sandwiches with slices of cheese and then added a few cuts of ham lunch meat to mine and Dominic's before topping them with another piece of buttered bread.

Dinner tonight was quick and easy—which I loved since today had been such a rough day at work, followed by more stress with Mikey's fight at school. I just wanted to eat and then relax for the rest of the night. So much so that I'd even grabbed paper plates, so we didn't have as many dishes.

I flipped the sandwiches and let them brown on the other side, enjoying the delicious aroma floating in the air around us. Sally was already sitting at the table, playing with Olivia as she sat on Dominic's lap and giggled at the funny faces Sally had made. Mikey had washed up and was sitting at the table too, but he wasn't interested in engaging anyone in conversation, which was apparent by the scowl on his face and the way his arms were folded over his chest.

"Dinner is ready," I said, setting down the plate filled with grilled cheese sandwiches that were cut in half for the kids. I slid a paper plate over to Dominic with his sandwich, then went back for mine.

The soup was sitting on the table, so I served bowls for the kids before offering Dominic one. Olivia was sitting in the highchair I had for when Penny came over, already devouring the sandwich he had cut into small pieces and given her.

I sat down and served myself a bowl of soup, then looked around the table, trying to force the idea out of my head that someday this could be my family, all together at the dinner table.

"So, overall, how was the first day back to school after spring break?" I asked, looking around the table since three of them could answer the question, and the silence was killing me.

Sally shrugged. Mikey rolled his eyes. And Dominic smiled softly, knowing how defeated that made me feel.

"It was nice to be back in the classroom and to hear everyone's stories about what they did on break," Dominic answered. "I especially loved hearing Mikey talk about his camping trip. Did you have fun too, Sally?"

She took a bite of grilled cheese and nodded.

"What was your favorite part?" I asked, hoping to pull Sally into the conversation.

"When grandpa tried to make s'mores and burned them," she giggled. "The marshmallow looked like it was on fire. Grandma wouldn't eat them and made us ice cream sundaes instead."

"Sounds like something he would do," I laughed. "I remember going camping with them when Abby and I were little, and he'd burn the hotdogs. Grandma liked them a little burnt, but he would straight up burn them to a crisp where they weren't edible anymore."

"Is that where you learned to burn food?" Sally asked, looking at me as she dipped a piece of her sandwich into her soup.

I was mid-sip, taking a drink of my iced tea, when I started to choke.

"I don't burn food," I objected, wiping my mouth with a napkin.

"Uh-huh. Remember the turkey at Thanksgiving?" Mikey said, finally joining in the conversation.

I pretended to give him a warning look which only spurred him to laugh. I couldn't be mad if I wanted to. Hearing his laughter was something that I'd missed, and I would take it any chance I got.

"That was one time," I countered, shaking my finger at him. "And it was an accident. Grandpa used to burn the hotdogs every single time until Grandma took his privileges away."

Dominic covered his mouth with his hand and laughed.

"So, what was your favorite part about camping, Mikey?" I asked, hoping he was still in a good mood to talk.

He shrugged and took a bite.

"I don't know. I guess putting up the tent with Grandpa. It

took us like ten times before he could get it to work, but we laughed every time it would fall down. He'd get mad and say bad words, but then I would laugh, and he wasn't mad anymore until it happened again. Finally, he got it up, and we hung out inside it while the girls had to stay in the RV."

"Sounds like fun," Dominic said. "I used to love doing that with my dad when I was young. We plan to do some camping trips with Olivia soon."

"Do your parents have an RV?" Sally asked around a mouthful of grilled cheese.

"Don't talk with your mouth full," I reminded her quietly, so I didn't embarrass her.

"No, but they're looking at buying one. They've been shopping for a while, but I think your grandparents finally have them sold on one. It's a lot bigger than they wanted, but then again, we need plenty of room to spread out without being on top of each other, so I guess it can't be too big."

"Did you build tents with your dad too?" Mikey asked, his attention solely focused on Dominic.

"I did. We used to go for the weekend and would set it up as soon as we got there. My dad always found the best camping spots with plenty of trees to hook things to. It was something he used to do with my grandpa before he passed. I spent a lot of my childhood outdoors, fishing and camping."

"Is that how you learned to fish so good?" Mikey questioned.

I leaned back in my chair and watched their exchange, noticing how Mikey hung on to every word Dominic said. It pulled at my heart, knowing how much he was missing out on this kind of bonding with his dad. I still needed to talk to the kids about Rick, but more importantly, I needed to speak to him about stepping up and being a better father.

"I'd like to think so," Dominic laughed. "I don't know that I'm *that* good at it, but it's something that I enjoy doing."

"Maybe you can go with us again sometime?" Sally asked, a sudden hopefulness in her voice.

"Umm, yeah," Dominic stuttered, looking to me for guidance.

I didn't want to get the kids too attached to the idea of constantly having Dominic around, nor did I want them to think that he was going to be part of our family. It was a hard line that I didn't want to cross, yet I couldn't stop the words from coming out of my mouth.

"Do you know what would be really fun?" I asked, grabbing everyone's attention—even Olivia as she clapped excitedly from her highchair. I smiled at her and then continued. "We should all borrow Grandma and Grandpa's RV this summer and go camping for a week. We can pick a spot by a lake to do some fishing, then make s'mores and tell scary stories in the dark with flashlights."

"Can we swim in the lake too, Mom?" Sally's eyes lit up.

"Of course! Maybe you and I can swim with Olivia while the guys fish and catch us some dinner?"

"That would be awesome!" Sally shrieked.

"Can we really do that?" Mikey asked, sounding afraid to get his hopes up.

"Of course we can. And if we can't borrow their RV that weekend, I'll rent one. It'll be fine. Maybe we can do it the first week after school is out? Start the summer off right!"

"We're in," Dominic said, giving me a look that sent butterflies through my stomach. "And I'm sure my parents will have their RV by then, so we'll have a backup option, just in case."

"Sounds perfect."

The kids spent the rest of dinner talking about what they wanted to do on our trip and what they were most excited about. My mind was racing, stressing over what I had just signed us up for, but my heart never felt fuller.

Eighteen
Dominic

Jane insisted that I go hang out in the living room with the kids while she cleaned up dinner. I wanted to object and force her to let me help, but something in her eyes made me reconsider. I knew she was already feeling nervous about anything happening between us, but the fact that she'd proposed we all go on a week-long camping trip together made me hopeful that she would give this thing a chance.

Olivia sat on the floor playing with Sally while Mikey sat in a chair, reading a book. Jane came out and joined us a few minutes later, sitting on the couch beside me.

"They play so well together," she commented, smiling at how gentle Sally was with Olivia.

"I worry Olivia is going to accidentally rip the head off that Barbie," I whispered through my teeth, only slightly turning my head toward her.

"It wouldn't be the first time, nor will it be the last. Don't worry; I have quite the collection of Barbie heads in the garage."

"Is that something I need to be worried about?" I teased. "Are you going to turn into one of those psycho girls who do strange things with them?"

"Guess you'll never know," she said with a wink. "Does

that make you reconsider going on a trip with us in a few months?"

I shrugged one shoulder, then leaned in and casually bumped her with it.

"I think I'm brave enough to handle you and some Barbie heads. I mean, I have seen you fish…"

She returned the bump with one of her own, and then suddenly, we were leaning into each other, our bodies almost close enough to be touching.

I wanted to say something or reach over and see if she'd let me hold her hand, but I didn't want to rush anything between us. Nor did I want the kids to find out about us until she was ready to tell them.

Her phone started to ring from the coffee table. She sighed heavily and then answered it, her brow creasing as she listened. I shifted my attention to the girls and picked up one of the extra Barbies, making her dance as Olivia giggled.

"Okay, please get her admitted and text me the room number. I'm on my way in a few minutes."

She hung up and pinched the bridge of her nose between her fingers.

"Everything alright?" I asked.

"It's the emergency I had earlier. One of my patients is being admitted to the hospital, and I need to go down to check on them and talk with the doctor. I'm sorry to cut the night early, you don't have to rush off, but I get it if you don't want to hang out with my parents," she laughed, pressing buttons on her phone.

"Your parents?"

"Yeah, they come watch the kids for me when I get called in. It doesn't happen often, but they know there's always a chance it can happen."

"Jane?"

"Yeah?"

She still hadn't looked up from her phone. I reached over and covered her hand with mine, forcing her to stop.

Her brown eyes found mine and paused for a moment.

"You don't need to call your parents. I'm happy to stay and watch the kids unless you don't want me to."

She pulled her head back in surprise.

"I don't want to take advantage of you being here. It's not a big deal to call them—"

"Jane, again, I don't mind. I enjoy spending time with them, and I'm already here. I've got this, go."

"Are you sure?"

I raised an eyebrow and cocked my head to the side.

"Okay, okay," she laughed. "Thank you. I appreciate your help, really."

"It's not a problem. We'll have fun and see you when you get back."

"Thank you. It shouldn't be too long. If you need anything, call Abby. She'll know what to do."

I nodded and winked at her when I knew the kids weren't looking.

She grabbed her stuff and headed out the door, leaving us alone.

I let the girls keep playing Barbies and shifted my attention to Mikey.

"Hey, what are you reading?" I asked, rubbing my hands together nervously, knowing there was a good chance he would ignore me or shut down my attempt to talk to him.

"It's *Temperamental Tom and the T-Rex*."

"What's it about?"

"This kid named Tom who has a bad temper and gets angry really easily. Whenever he gets mad, he has to find his best friend, the T-Rex, to help him calm down."

"That sounds fun," I said. "How does the T-Rex help him?"

"Different ways. Sometimes they go for a walk, sometimes they chase lizards, and sometimes they throw rocks into the lake. Different things, but the best part is that no one else can see the T-Rex. Just Tom. When he can't handle things, he gets to go on these crazy adventures with T-Rex."

"I wish I would have had a book like that growing up," I said. "I always got in trouble for fighting in school because I couldn't control my temper."

Mikey suddenly stopped, lowered the book to his lap, and looked at me.

"You used to get into fights too?"

"Well, not all the time. But a handful of times."

"What for?"

"Little things here and there. But most of them were because I was trying to protect someone I cared about."

Something changed in Mikey's eyes, and I felt the change in the energy in the room.

"Like who?"

"Well, my mom, for one. Growing up, I was always close to my parents, and kids would make fun of me for being a momma's boy. They'd tease me about not having any other friends and that my mom was only my friend because she felt bad for me. Then it changed, and they'd start making fun of her. That's when I would get in fights, trying to defend her."

"Did they stop?"

I shook my head and laughed.

"No. They didn't. But that's the thing about bullies— it doesn't matter how many fights you get into with them, they don't stop. Unless an adult steps in and does something to stop them, it's just a vicious cycle."

"So what did you do?"

"I started listening to my parents and ignored them. I didn't give them the attention they were looking for. I walked away when they tried to start a fight. Soon, they got bored and just stopped."

He studied me for a moment and then looked down at Sally and Olivia.

"So, that's what I should do? Just ignore them?"

I nodded and smiled at him.

"I would. But also talk to your mom. Let her know what's going on. I used to keep my mom from finding out what was happening because I didn't want her feelings to get hurt. But then I was getting into so much trouble at school for fighting that I didn't have any choice. She sat me down and told me that she loved me for wanting to defend her but that their words didn't bother her. She told me that in life, we're going to have people who don't like us and who make fun of us. While it sucks, you don't have to give them attention. Find the people who like you and make you feel good about yourself and give your attention to them instead."

He set his book on the end table beside him and looked at me.

"I didn't like him making fun of Sally," he admitted.

"I know. And you're a great big brother for wanting to stand up for her. But at the end of the day, who cares whether she still plays with Barbies? Or if you join her? That's such a silly thing to waste time on, and I feel bad that he has nothing better to do than to pick on someone for how they decide to play. If you guys are having fun, that's all that matters."

"I guess so."

"Well, I don't know about you, but I think it's fun. In fact, I was going to sit down and play Barbies with the girls. Wanna join us?"

He chewed his nail for a moment, then got up.

"Alright, but I'm getting my superheroes."

A few minutes later, he returned from his room with a handful of Barbie-sized dolls ranging from The Hulk to

Spiderman to Captain America. I was impressed with how good of condition they were in, but even more that he was willing to let Sally and Olivia play with them too.

He offered me the first pick on who I wanted to be, so I chose Iron Man and a Barbie with bright pink hair. Mikey decided to be The Hulk and grabbed a Barbie with short black hair, one that Sally had cut one day when Jane wasn't looking, according to the story he told me.

Olivia was excited about toys in general so she wanted all of them and constantly tried to stick their heads in her mouth. Sally laughed and gave her Spider-Man while she kept Captain America for herself.

I don't know how long we played, but I couldn't remember the last time I'd had so much fun. I was so lost in the moment that I hadn't heard my phone when Jane texted to let me know she was on her way home, nor did I hear her come in. I looked up and found her watching us as she leaned against the wall, a beautiful smile on her face.

Nineteen
Jane

It had been almost three weeks since I'd invited Dominic and Olivia over for dinner. After I saw him on the floor playing Barbies with my kids, my heart was gone, forever tied to that image. Since then, we'd shared a few more meals together and they were a regular part of our Saturday night pizza nights.

The thoughts of getting too close to him were starting to fade, and I realized that the kids would be attached to him regardless of whether I dated him. Even if I didn't invite them over when it was just the kids and me, he was still hanging out at Abby and Nate's house. Heck, he'd even gone with Nate for a couple of guys' nights out. It was great to see him interacting with others and making some friends in town.

I stood in line at Surf 'N Shack, waiting to pick up dinner for the kids and me since I was too tired to bother with cooking tonight. Plus, it was Friday night, and we could all use a treat. My parents had picked them up from school and were working on some crafts for Easter while I grabbed the food after work.

There were only a few people ahead of me, and the smell of fried food permeated the air, sending my stomach growling.

By the time I got to the register, the woman who was working it gave me a quick smile and then rushed off as Capshaw took her place.

"Enjoy your lunch," he called to her. "Hey, Jane. What can I get for you?"

It had been over a year since Capshaw and I had dated—if you could even call it that. It was more like friends with benefits, though we never really explored the friendship part. He was basically a great hook-up, and I took advantage of it as often as I could until we got caught.

"Hi," I said warmly. "Can I get the family bucket, please? And instead of the coleslaw, can I substitute extra hush puppies?"

"Of course. Anything else?"

"That's it." I smiled and waited while he entered everything into the computer.

"So, how have you been?" he asked, looking up at me briefly before pushing more buttons.

"Good, busy," I laughed. "The kids keep me on my toes. Before I know it, summer break will be here. How are you?"

He shrugged his shoulders, and a grin snuck across his cheeks along with a faint blush.

"Good, can't complain."

"Mmm hmm," I teased. "Nate mentioned that you seemed happy a few weeks ago. Might this have something to do with a woman?"

He looked over his shoulder and then back at me.

"Maybe."

I smiled widely, genuinely pleased for him.

"Well, that's amazing, Capshaw. I'm really excited for you and glad that you've found someone who makes you this happy." I handed him my card and waited while he rang me up.

"Thanks, Jane, I appreciate that."

He handed me back my card and the receipt to sign. I said goodbye and moved to the side to wait for my order. It was good to see him so excited about something, and I felt like I could relate because that was how I felt lately every time I was around Dominic and Olivia.

****

"Do you have your shoes on? We need to get going," I called down the hallway as I pushed the earring through my ear and then ran my hands down the front of my dress to smooth it.

"You don't have to yell. I'm right here," Mikey said, standing beside me.

"Thank you, but I was talking to your sister. You look nice, very handsome." I reached down and adjusted the collar of his light blue buttoned-down shirt. We didn't dress up often, but Easter Sunday was the one day we were expected to.

"Sally, let's go."

I looked at my watch and grimaced. If we didn't get in the car in the next five minutes, we would be late getting to my parent's house, and the last thing I needed today was a lecture on tardiness from my mother. I was too tired for that, though I was exhausted most days lately.

A few minutes later, Sally came out of her bedroom with a frown as she held up two different shoes.

"These don't match."

"No, they don't. Come on, let's go find the right ones so we can get going. If we're late, I'm telling Grandma it's all your fault."

"Mom! You can't do that," she objected.

"Well then, we'd better hurry." I swatted her butt as she rushed in front of me and went straight to her closet, where her shoes were all piled together in one giant mess.

"Do I even want to know?" I asked, pinching the bridge of my nose between two fingers.

"I wanted to wear the ones with the glitter."

"Fine, let's start looking. Mikey, get in here and help, please."

I'd never seen shoes fly through the air as fast as they did as we all worked together to find Sally's missing shoe. The mess would have to wait until we got home, but for now, we had both shoes. I left her to put them on while I grabbed my coffee and purse from the kitchen.

"Alright, you guys, let's go! You have thirty seconds to get your little butts into the car before I leave without you."

They quickly shuffled past me, mumbling something under their breath that I didn't have the time to try to hear. We packed into the car and raced over to my parent's house.

By the time we got there, Abby and Nate had just pulled up and were getting Penny out of her car seat.

"I'm glad we weren't the only ones running behind," I said as I hugged Abby and gently pinched Penny's cheeks.

"Well, Penny threw up on me, which made me throw up, so we were running late after we all had to change clothes."

I scrunched my nose and held the front door open for Mikey and Sally to go inside.

"Why did she throw up? Is she not feeling well?"

"I'm not sure. She was fine all morning, and then suddenly, she just started getting sick."

"I'll take a look at her once we get inside," I assured her, holding the door open as I waited for Nate to catch up with the bags of groceries he had hanging from his arms.

"Good morning," he said, leaning in to kiss my cheek before darting inside. "Happy Easter."

"Happy Easter to you, too," I replied, pulling the door shut behind me.

Mikey and Sally had already brought our stuff inside and taken it to the kitchen, where my mom was probably already going through everything and judging what I had bought. While she was overall better this past year after going on a much needed trip with my dad, she was still my mom, and it was always difficult for Abby and me to earn her approval, especially with Easter dinner. I never understood why she didn't just cook it all herself if she was going to spend the entire day complaining about what we'd done wrong.

I walked into the kitchen and hugged my dad before moving around the island to greet my mom.

"Happy Easter," I said, plastering a fake smile on my face as she barely wrapped her arm around to embrace me.

"Yes, Happy Easter to you too, dear. I see you've brought the stuff to make the ham but haven't started yet?" She arched an eyebrow at me before looking down at the ingredients sitting on the island that she'd pulled from the bags.

"I didn't have time to start it before I left. But not to worry, it's precooked and will be ready when it's time to eat."

"Precooked?"

"Yes."

"As in...."

"As in, someone else cooked it before I bought it so I didn't have to spend the extra time cooking it today."

Her eyes narrowed with disapproval. Whether it was my sarcasm or the damn ham, who knew.

"Well, alright then."

"Breakfast is ready," my dad said, interrupting my mother before she could continue. "Let's all sit down and enjoy it before it gets cold."

Abby got Penny situated in her highchair and then took a seat in the corner. I glared at her and she shrugged her shoulders as if she didn't know that was my go-to spot when I was trying to avoid our mother.

I pulled out the seat next to Sally and sat down, already feeling stiff with tension knowing that my mother would be taking the seat beside me. My father always sat at the head of the table, and she always sat right next to him.

We bowed our heads and said grace before the plates were passed around the table. Everyone was quiet as we served ourselves, except for Abby, who was making an odd moaning noise in the corner. I glanced over and noticed her plate was filled with a handful of slices of bacon, and her eyes were closed as she practically devoured the piece in her hand.

"Abby," Nate hissed as quietly as possible, trying to get her attention.

Her eyes opened slowly as her fingers pushed the last bit into her mouth.

"Hmm?"

"You're umm…" He rubbed his lips together nervously as he thought about how to answer her. "You're…."

"Moaning," my mother blurted out.

Abby's face turned bright red as she covered her face with her hands.

"I don't think I've seen you enjoy bacon that much since you were preg—" My words died in my throat, unable to come out.

My mind was racing as the word *pregnant* floated around it, taunting and teasing me. I finished my birth control last week and should have started this past Tuesday, but I didn't. I started doing the math in my head, counting back how many weeks it had been since Dominic and I had sex. It had only been one time, but the condom had broken, so I couldn't entirely rule out the possibility that I could be pregnant. That would explain a lot right now—like why I was constantly so tired and my boobs hurt.

"Are you?" Nate asked, his eyes lit up with hope.

"Umm, I don't think so."

"You'd think *Jane* was the one who could be knocked up with the panicked look on her face," my mother snorted.

I tried to school my features the best I could because the last thing I needed right now was anybody taking my mom seriously. I needed to calm down and take a test. That was the only way to know what was really going on. Until then, I had to keep my shit together and not alert anyone to the panic attack I was having deep inside.

Thankfully, Sally switched the conversation to the tooth she'd recently lost and how the tooth fairy had given her $12 for it instead of the usual $3. I'd been so exhausted that I hadn't taken the time to thoroughly look at all of the bills I'd pulled out of my wallet and gave her a ten-dollar bill, along with two ones.

After we finished breakfast, we all went to church, then came back to my parent's house and took the kids outside for an Easter egg hunt. That was my father's favorite part of the holiday; he was always as giddy as the kids. This year would be even more fun now that Penny could walk and search for them with Mikey and Sally.

Abby and I walked around the yard, laughing as the kids ran off, excited when they spotted the first few eggs and added them to their baskets. I lingered behind, focusing on the cobblestone path that led to the garden, my mind still distracted.

The kids ran around looking for more eggs while I stressed over whether mine had been fertilized.

"Hey, what's going on with you?" Abby said, walking up beside me and bumping shoulders.

"Nothing," I lied, keeping my eyes averted from hers so she couldn't see the truth behind them.

"You're a shitty liar. I could tell something was up the second mom mentioned you looked freaked out about someone being pregnant."

I blew out a breath and watched as Sally stopped to help Penny get an egg that she couldn't reach. It reminded me of how she was with Olivia, and that made my heart flutter in an odd way.

"So, are you?"

"Am I what?" I asked, still refusing to look at her.

"Are you pregnant?"

I stopped dead in my tracks and froze.

"Oh my God!" she gasped, yanking my arm and swinging me around to face her. "You are, aren't you?!"

"I don't know," I hissed, looking around to see if anyone was watching us. "But keep your voice down, please. I don't need anyone else knowing about this."

"Is it Dominic's?"

"First, we don't even know for sure that I'm pregnant," I said, sidestepping her question.

"Did you sleep with him?"

I felt my skin prickle as the blush crept over it.

"You totally did!" Her eyes widened as a grin started spreading over her face.

"Will you be quiet," I pleaded, lowering my head.

"Hurry, laugh."

I looked up at her, confused, and then saw my mother watching us from across the yard.

I tipped my head back and laughed as Abby joined me. We'd done it since we were teenagers when we wanted to keep something from her.

We continued our routine for a few minutes until my mom turned her attention to something else.

"Okay, spill it," Abby said, her tone now serious. "Did you sleep with him?"

"Yes," I whispered, looking around to make sure no one was close enough to hear.

"And now you might be pregnant?"

"I don't know," I sighed heavily, my shoulders rising and falling heavily. "Maybe."

"Maybe?"

"The condom broke," I muttered lowly.

Her eyes widened, and for a moment, I was worried they might pop out of her head.

"Have you taken a test?"

"No. It wasn't even on my radar until I mentioned you eating so much bacon at breakfast." I turned to face her head-on. "Which, by the way—are you pregnant?"

"I don't know." She shrugged. "It's a possibility."

"Are you guys officially trying?"

"We're not *not* trying."

"Abby!" I squealed excitedly, then pulled my emotion back when my dad glanced our way. "That's so exciting! I'm so happy for you guys!"

"We don't even know if I'm pregnant yet."

"I bet you are." I laughed and pointed a finger at her. "You only eat bacon like that when you're knocked up."

The kids were getting close to being done with the egg hunt, which meant that we would all be heading inside, and the women would be getting started on dinner.

"Only one way to know for sure." She gave me a look that had me a bit worried.

<u>Twenty</u>
Jane

"Damn it, the butter is bad," Abby said, slamming the refrigerator door closed and leaning her arm against it. "Jane and I are going to run to the grocery store to get some. We'll be back shortly."

My mother pulled her brows together as she walked over and pushed Abby out of the way. She opened the door and pulled out the butter, lowering her glasses to her eyes as she read the label.

"It says best by today. It's fine."

"I'm not willing to trust it," Abby replied with her hands on her hips. "I'm not going to be responsible for everyone getting sick on Easter from mashed potatoes made with expired butter."

"It'll be fine," my mother argued. "No one has ever gotten sick from bad butter."

"Ha!" Abby snorted. "Jane has to deal with sick kids all the time. Ask her how many come in from butter toxification."

I wrinkled my brow and gave her my best *what the fuck are you talking about* look while my mom's head was turned the other way. She pinned me with her own that said *just go with it.*

"I highly doubt that," Mother continued.

"It's true," I lied. "You wouldn't believe the number of sick kids I see from butter toxification. It's not something you want to risk with Penny being as young as she is."

My mom folded her arms over her chest and looked at both of us as if we'd lost our damn minds—which we had.

"Fine. Go to the store but make it quick. This dinner isn't going to make itself."

Sure it is because you don't ever step back and actually let anyone do anything. You just bark orders at them until they either give up and quit or they do it your way.

"I'll be back soon, be good." I patted Mikey on his head and smiled at him and Sally.

Once we were outside, I waited by the passenger door while Abby fumbled with the key fob to unlock the truck. We climbed inside and rode in silence to the grocery store.

I grabbed a handheld basket and headed straight to the aisle we needed, not wanting to be here a second longer than we had to. Abby rushed off to grab a package of diapers and promised to meet me in a few minutes. I was so focused on studying each of the tests that I hadn't heard anyone walk up beside me.

"Get the three-pack. You're going to want to make sure," Abby said, reaching over and grabbing two boxes. She dropped one in my basket and one in hers. "Here, get this set too. I like to get at least two or three different brands, just to be sure."

She added a few more packages to my basket.

"Did you need anything else?" she asked, totally calm as

if it were every day that we stocked up on pregnancy tests together.

"I don't think so."

"Alright, well, I have to grab some butter, so I'll get that and meet you at the register."

I nodded and turned the opposite way before deciding to grab some chocolate. If there was anything in life that could make me feel better, it was chocolate.

The store was relatively quiet, given that it was the only one in Beaumont Creek open on Easter. I grabbed a few chocolate bars and tossed them in my basket, laughing at how ridiculous it looked with the boxes of pregnancy tests stacked high.

I rounded the corner to head to the registers when suddenly someone came around the other aisle and almost hit me.

"Sorry," Dominic apologized, his eyes immediately lighting up when he saw me. His hand reached out and steadied me around the waist, the touch electrifying.

"No, it's my fault. I wasn't paying attention. Again." I laughed nervously.

"Don't worry about it. You here by yourself?"

He glanced down at the handheld basket on my arm, and I noticed the way his features suddenly changed. His jaw tightened, and his eyebrows rose slightly when he saw the pregnancy tests.

"I'm here with Abby," I rushed out, hoping I could get away before he could ask any more questions. "I'm actually meeting her at the register, so I better go."

But before I could get away, I heard Abby's voice behind me.

"Hey, Dominic!"

He stepped away from me slightly as she leaned on her tiptoes to hug him.

"Happy Easter!"

"Yeah, you too." His voice was edgy and guarded.

"What brings you to the supermarket on Easter?" she asked, apparently completely oblivious to the basket full of pregnancy tests that suddenly felt like they weighed a hundred pounds hanging from my arm.

"I came to grab a few things for my mom," he answered, looking back at me with a question I couldn't quite read in his eyes.

"Same for us," Abby replied cheerfully.

He glanced down at the basket she was holding, his eyebrow slightly rising again as he noticed the boxes of pregnancy tests mixed in with the diapers and butter.

"I see. Well, I won't keep you, ladies."

Abby looked between us, suddenly noticing the tension.

"I'm, um, I'm gonna go ahead and go to the checkout. I'll meet you there in a few, Jane?"

"Sounds good," I answered but kept my eyes on Dominic as she walked away.

We stood there for a few seconds in awkward silence until he finally broke it.

"I don't want to be rude or overstep here, Jane, so I apologize in advance. But is there something we need to talk about?" He nodded to the tests.

"Nope, we're good," I lied. "Abby and Nate have been trying to get pregnant, so she decided to stock up on tests. I'm holding these ones for her since her basket was too full."

I didn't bother to explain why we weren't smart enough to grab a full-sized shopping cart if everything in both of our baskets were hers, to begin with.

He rubbed his lips together and studied me.

"Okay. Well, I'll let you go. It was nice seeing you."

"You too."

I debated whether or not to lean in and hug him, but the way his shoulders squared suggested that maybe I shouldn't. Instead, I pulled my shoulders back and headed to the cash register without looking back.

After we got back to the house, Abby made small talk with my mother about butter toxification—which I lectured her about not being a real word on our way home—while I sat with the kids for a few minutes and had them show me the crafts they had made with my parents.

We had some time to kill before we needed to start dinner, so I went and hung out upstairs with Abby while she got Penny down for a nap. Once she was tucked into her Pack 'N Play, Abby and I took the baby monitor and snuck into the bathroom that joined the two rooms that used to be ours.

Abby opened the bag of tests we'd bought and then pulled out two disposable cups she'd snuck up from the kitchen and set them on the counter. We looked at each other and then began ripping the boxes open. There wasn't much time before someone would come looking for us, so we had to make it fast.

We took turns peeing in the cups and then lined them up beside each other. I'd done a lot of stressful things in my life, but at the moment, this one ranked as one of the highest.

"You ready?" she asked.

I nodded, then took the cap off the stick and lowered it into the cup. She did the same, then we placed the caps on the tests and set the tests down on the other side of the sink in the same order as the cups. We did a few more, then froze when we heard our mother calling for us.

Abby spun around, panic on her face as she looked at me.

"What do we do?" she whispered.

"I'll sneak out and tell her you're trying to get Penny down."

"Okay."
I tried to move around her in the small space of the bathroom and cringed when I felt my butt hit one of the cups. Abby gasped and reached for it, grabbing it before it could spill.

"Jane? Abby?" Mother called.

"Go!" She waved her hand to shoo me out of the bathroom.

I inhaled deeply, opened the door, and came face to face with my mother.

"Hey, Mom."

"What are you doing up here?"

"Mikey was in the other bathroom, and I really had to go, so I came up to use this one."

"Where's your sister?"

"I think she's in her room trying to get Penny down for a nap."

"Oh, right. I remember she mentioned that. Well, we better get back down there and be quiet so poor Penny can sleep. Let's go."

She linked her arm in mine and led me down the stairs.

We were almost to the bottom when I suddenly pulled away.

"Crap, I left my phone in the bathroom. I better go get it."

She rolled her eyes and headed to the kitchen while I scurried back up the stairs. I opened the bathroom door and found Abby staring at the tests with her hand covering her mouth.

"What? What's the matter?" I asked, closing the door behind me.

"When you knocked the cup over, I grabbed it but didn't see which one it was. And now I don't know which side it's supposed to go on."

"Okay," I said slowly. "So, what's the problem?"

"The problem is that one of us is pregnant, and I don't know who."

Twenty-One
Dominic

"Alright, let's open our books to chapter ten. Mikey, can you read the first paragraph for us?"

I sat on the edge of my desk, resting the book on my thigh while I tried to listen to him read, but my mind was focused elsewhere. Primarily, it was on his mother and whether or not she might be pregnant. It had been two days since I'd run into her at the store with her basket full of pregnancy tests, yet I couldn't bring myself to reach out to her to ask what I really wanted to know.

But then again, I reminded myself that it wasn't any of my business. She'd insisted that the tests were for Abby, and I knew that she and Nate were trying to get pregnant again. So it made sense. That still didn't help the nagging feeling that reminded me that the condom broke the night we had sex over four weeks ago. While Jane confirmed that she was on birth control, I knew there could still be a chance that she could be pregnant. Plus, the way she acted when she saw me made me feel as if there was something she wasn't telling me and that those tests might have been for her. Why else would they have two handheld baskets instead of just getting a shopping cart if everything was Abby's?

I felt eyes on me and looked up to find the entire class watching me.

"Great job," I said, clearing my throat and having no idea whether or not Mikey actually read what I asked him to.

"Maddie, can you read the next one for us?"

I needed to clear my head and focus, no matter how hard it was.

After we got through five students reading out loud, I decided to shift gears and have them read the rest quietly to themselves. My head was pounding, and I was looking forward to the day being over. Not that the evening would be any better, but at least I could be at home cuddling with Olivia while obsessing over Jane and whether I had accidentally knocked her up.

The rest of the day was painfully long as the students acted up and I had to break up more fights than usual. I was exhausted by the time the bell rang and debated on whether to stick around and grade papers or call it a day and go home.

My phone dinged with a text message alert, so I picked it up and checked it, hoping it was from Jane.

I frowned when I saw Rebecca's name on the screen, wondering what my ex-wife wanted now. It was probably for money so she could get her next fix; that was always her aim.

Rebecca: Hey, can we meet up soon to talk?

I didn't bother to reply, just deleted the message and shoved my phone into my pocket. It had been a long day, and her message sent me further into a bad mood, so I packed my stuff up and headed out.

Once I got home, I took a quick shower to wash the day off of me. My mom confirmed that Olivia was still down for her nap and that she would text me when she was up.

I rubbed the back of my neck, feeling the knots from the tension that was constantly building. Not only was I stressed about not knowing if Jane was pregnant and hiding it from me, but I had the added stress of Rebecca's text combined with the frustration of not being able to touch Jane since that night. There was a lot building up, and I needed a fucking release.

The water was hot as it sprayed across my back, pelting the knots I desperately wanted to get rid of. I closed my eyes and relaxed, allowing the stress to melt away. It felt so good that I lost track of how long I'd been standing there.

For just a brief moment, I allowed myself to replay the memories of that night with Jane: the way she looked as she came, how she tasted, and how soft her skin was as my tongue trailed across it. I shuddered when I remembered the feel of her pussy as it clenched my cock, wrapping so tightly around it as she milked every drop of my orgasm out of me.

I squirted some body wash into my hand and lathered it all over myself, moaning when I got to my rock-hard cock. My hand gripped it tightly, slathering the gel across it as I imagined Jane kneeling in front of me as she pulled me so far into the back of her throat that she couldn't take anymore.

I pumped faster, my balls aching for a release, but I wasn't going to give in that easily. If Jane were here, I'd have her suck me until every last drop was swallowed. Then I'd take her to the bedroom and lay her on my bed where I would tie her legs to the bedposts, keeping her in place while I buried my face between her legs, eating her sweet pussy until she came on my face.

That thought alone was almost my undoing as I licked my lips, pretending that I could taste her on them. I wasn't sure that I would ever get enough of going down on her, but then again, watching my dick slide in and out of her as we fucked in front of the mirror was another favorite of mine too.

Everything about Jane was incredible, and I wanted more. I wanted more from the moment I'd pulled out of her. Had the condom not broken that night and soured the mood, I would have tried going for a round two with her after we got some carbs in us.

Jane rode me perfectly. Her body connected with mine as if we were meant to be together—maybe in more ways than one, but I refused to allow myself to think about that. But I also couldn't stop obsessing over how great the sex had been with her.

I gripped my cock tighter, pumping harder as I held one hand against the wall to brace myself. My heart was racing as I panted, so close to coming. I closed my eyes tighter, picturing Jane's face as her lips parted, a moan escaping as she came. That image alone was enough to make me blow my load.

My breathing grew more rapid as I jerked myself off, spraying ropes of cum across the shower tiles. I grunted and kept going until I had nothing left.

Twenty-Two

Jane

I continued staring at the two pink lines as I chewed my nail nervously. Out of four tests, two were positive, and two looked drunk with only parts of the line showing up but so faint that you couldn't tell what they were trying to say. They were all lined up along the bathroom counter, the first chance I had to take them since Sunday at my parent's house when the cups got mixed up.

Monday the kids were home from school because of the holiday and got up earlier than I expected, which left me no time to take one. Then by that night, I was too exhausted to bother, so I threw myself in bed instead.

Tuesday had started out rushed, with all of us trying to remember how to function and get out of the door on time, so that was a no-go from the start. It seemed my days were constantly busy and there was never enough time to stop and do what I needed to. Or maybe there was time, I just couldn't take it without having to explain to the kids what I was doing. And Lord knew I wasn't ready to have that conversation with them just yet about possibly being pregnant with Dominic's baby. Where would I even start?

So, that brought us to Wednesday when I'd gotten the kids to school on time and arrived to work with a few minutes to spare. Sure, I'd skipped stopping by Rockin' Rooster for coffee, but some things were more important. Like, finding out that I was possibly knocked up on hump day— what an odd coincidence, wasn't it? I humped a hot, single father that I should have stayed away from, and now I was possibly carrying his child.

I looked down at my phone, noticing the time. The first patient of the day would be ready soon, so I needed to get out there. I grabbed the tests from the counter, put them back into the boxes they came from, and then shoved them into my purse. They'd have to live there until I could go home and throw them away. I couldn't risk anyone accidentally stumbling upon them here.

I looked in the mirror, noticing the dark circles under my eyes. I wished I could go home and crawl back into bed, but I couldn't. However, I could go for a cup of coffee at this point. Even if I were pregnant, one cup would be okay. I made a quick note to schedule an appointment with my doctor to request the bloodwork to confirm whether or not I was expecting.

After I tucked my purse into the bottom drawer of my desk, I smoothed down the dress I was wearing and tried to force myself to get focused. I was forty-two years old and had two kids already; one more wasn't going to kill me. Though Mikey might when he found out I was having his teacher's baby. Or my parents when they realized what I'd been doing with a guy that I wasn't even officially dating.

Shaking my head to clear my thoughts, I walked out of my office and headed to the front desk to grab the chart for the first patient I'd be seeing today.

"Good morning, Doctor Hughes," Nick said, smiling as he

slid around me to grab one of the other charts.

"Good morning, Nick. How are you?"

"Great, thank you. I'm heading in to do the vitals in room 1, and then you can go in."

"Okay. I'll grab some coffee then."

"There's a fresh pot," Sabrina said as she sat down around the desk. "Also, Ms. Gustavo canceled this morning. They rescheduled for next week instead. She was feeling ill and didn't want to get anyone here sick."

"That was nice of her. I appreciate that."

"And the hot single dad is in room 2," she added with wiggly eyebrows.

"Dominic?" His name got caught in my throat as I tried to get it out.

"Yup. Olivia was running a fever this morning, so he brought her in. We were able to give him Ms. Gustavo's spot since they called back-to-back."

"Sounds good," I replied, suddenly not feeling so good. I wasn't ready to see or talk to Dominic yet, especially not knowing for sure if I was pregnant. Granted, I knew that the two positive tests should be enough to convince me that I was, but there was this part of me that was afraid to accept it and was clinging to the wonky tests that looked inconclusive. For now, I was going with the uncertainty and wanted to be 100% sure before I said anything.

I went to the breakroom and fixed myself a cup of coffee, taking a few sips to try to get myself to wake up. It was going to be a long day.

After the first patient, my stomach was a ball of emotions as I knocked on the door to the room Dominic and Olivia were in. As I stepped inside, all of that faded away when I locked eyes with Olivia and she reached for me.

"Good morning," I said softly, closing the door behind me. She was still reaching for me, so I held out my hands and took her. "I heard she's running a fever this morning."

"Yeah, she was fine last night, but this morning she woke up cranky and felt warm. I checked her a few times and it kept showing 102-103. I thought it was best to bring her in."

"Of course. Let's see if we can figure out what's going on. Has she been coughing, sneezing, throwing up?" I looked up at him, and my stomach somersaulted again.

"She's had a bit of a runny nose, but I figured it might be allergies since everything is in bloom."

"It definitely could be. How's she eating?"

He waved his hand back and forth and scrunched his face.

"She's eating but doesn't seem to have the same appetite as before."

"Well, a stomach bug has been going around, so she might have gotten it."

I sat her on the table and played with her for a few minutes before I began examining her. I checked her lungs, listening to make sure they were clear and that I didn't hear any wheezing, then moved to her stomach.

Everything sounded good, so I checked her chart again, noticing she still had a fever when Nick scanned her. I looked down at her and saw her tugging on her ear before she started crying. I had been so distracted by Dominic that I had missed looking at her ears and had only focused on her nose and throat since he'd mentioned that she'd had a runny nose.

"Has she been pulling on her ears lately?" I asked, leaning closer to look inside.

"Not much that I've seen, but maybe a few times."

I immediately noticed inflammation and a small amount of pus in the middle ear.

"It looks like she has an ear infection in this ear," I said, pointing to it before moving to the other side to check her other ear. "It's common for children to get them, and hers doesn't look too bad at this time so I don't want to rush to give her antibiotics. Most of the time, the body can fight off middle ear infections on its own; however, if this lasts longer than 2-3 days, I want you to bring her back so I can see her and we can get some antibiotics started."

He nodded and I could see the worry on his face.

"In the meantime, it's important for her to rest and drink plenty of fluids. Water is fine, but I recommend supplementing with some Pedialyte to keep her from getting dehydrated. Tylenol will work well for reducing her fever as well as helping with the pain. She'll likely continue to be fussy and irritable, and she may have trouble sleeping. If you can get her to lay on her other side, that will help to keep from irritating this side," I said, gently rubbing her back as she started to cry again.

"Okay, thank you. I've already called in today, so I'll get her home and comfortable, then see if my mom can go grab some supplies."

I smiled, not ready to let go of her, but I knew I had to. I lifted her off of the table and handed her to Dominic.

"If anything changes or she worsens, please call me immediately. The Tylenol should break the fever, but if it gets any higher, please get her to the emergency room so they can get an IV started and monitor her."

"Will do."

An awkward silence permeated the air, both of us wanting to say more, but neither acted on it. I smiled and held the door open as he walked out, trying to ignore the pain it left behind when he did. I knew that I should have mentioned something to him about the positive pregnancy test, but I didn't want to talk about it until I knew for sure. Plus, he already had a lot going on with Olivia.

Twenty-Three
Dominic

The house was a mess, but Olivia was finally sleeping on my chest after being fussy most of the day. Jane was right about her having difficulty resting and no matter what position she was in, she couldn't seem to get comfortable. Finally, I gave in and cuddled her to me, forgetting everything else as I held her and prayed that she would feel better soon.

We'd been in the same spot on the couch for hours. I was starving, but I wasn't willing to risk her waking up if I tried to move her. So, I stayed put, ignoring the growls of my stomach for a little while longer.

I kept my phone charging on the table beside me, making sure I had it handy in case the substitute teacher needed anything from me today. I hated calling in, but my daughter came first. I'd already let the school know that I would be out for the rest of the week, which thankfully was only two more days. They'd been able to get the same sub to cover those days, and I'd agreed to be on call for whatever they needed.

Aside from my mom checking in on Olivia, my phone had been quiet all day. I'd put it on vibrate so it wouldn't wake her since she'd finally fallen asleep. I heard a soft vibrating noise and reached behind me, fumbling as I finally found it and picked it up.

I was thankful for wireless chargers. Just the movement of trying to grab it had caused Olivia to squirm and fuss a little bit until I patted her back softly and got her back to sleep. Once she was situated, I swiped my finger along the screen to unlock it and found a text message in the group thread between me, Nate, Abby, and Jane.

Nate: Anyone want to grab some wings and beer tonight at O'Sullivan's?

Jane: I can't tonight, but thanks for the offer.

Abby: Don't be a party pooper. Just come for dinner. It's one less thing you'll have to do tonight.

Jane: That would be great if there weren't a hundred things already on that list.

Abby: Like what?

Jane: Helping the kids with their homework, getting them fed, making them take showers, cleaning up the house, doing the laundry I didn't get to on Sunday. It's a never-ending list, sis.

Nate: Homework is overrated. The laundry will be there later. And most kids are stinky anyway. There— problems solved.

Jane: It's not that easy.

Nate: Dominic, can you excuse Mikey from having to turn in his homework tomorrow?

Me: Sorry, I'm not there this week. Olivia has an ear infection, so I'm home with her. I can't make it tonight either, but thanks for the invite.

Nate: (Person flipping desk GIF)

Abby: Calm down, you big caveman. You can still get your damn wings.

Nate: You'd have a different attitude if we were talking about bacon.

Abby: Mmmmm…. Bacon.

Nate: See?

Jane: It looks like you guys are having a date night tonight. Enjoy!

Nate: No can do. We have Penny.

Jane: So???

Abby: Nate doesn't like to do date nights when we have Penny. He says he can't get in the mood to be romantic with her there. So we have regular family nights out, but it's not a "date night".

Jane: You guys are so weird.

Nate: Hey, it's a thing. If I'm taking Abby out for a date, I want to be able to go *all in*.

Abby: Eew. Don't be gross. My sister is reading this.

Jane: (nauseous face emoji)

Nate: I won't apologize for who I am (hands up emoji)

Abby: Dominic, how is Olivia feeling? Do you need anything?

Jane: How's Olivia? Did her fever break?

Nate: It's so weird how you sisters are always in tune. Your messages literally came in at the same time.

Me: She's doing okay. I finally got her to sleep, but she's lying on my chest and if I try to move, she wakes up.

Jane: It's great that she's getting rest. What can we do to help you?

Nate: How are you going to help if you don't have time to go have beer and wings with us?

Jane: A sick child is more important than food, Nate. (Tongue sticking out emoji)

Abby: Or maybe she wants to see Dominic and not you.

Nate: Ouch. That hurts, you know.

Nate: Who wouldn't want to see me?

Abby: Not everything is about you…

Me: I'm good, guys but thank you.

Abby: What are you doing for dinner?

Me: I'm not sure yet. Right now, I just want her to get some rest. I'll worry about eating later.

Abby: We'll be there in an hour. And don't worry, I love baby cuddles, so she can sleep on me while you eat. Do you like wings? We can bring something else. Maybe something from Surf 'N Shack?

Me: You don't have to do that. I'm fine, I promise.

Jane: He likes the fried catfish meal with extra hush puppies. I'll bring some applesauce for Olivia. Maybe we can get her to eat that.

Abby: What do you and the kids want?

Jane: We'll do our usual. I'll give you cash when I get there.

Me: Guys—really, you don't have to do this.

Nate: I would stop trying to fight it, Dom. Have you met the Hughes women? They're impossible to stop once they have their mind set on something.

Jane: I'll meet you guys at Dominic's house in an hour.

Abby: Sounds good. We'll call in the order and be there soon.

Me: Wait—how do you guys even know where I live???

I waited a few minutes for a response, but none ever came. I'd been to Jane's house plenty of times, but she'd never been to mine.

Me: Hello? Should I be afraid?

Twenty-Four
Jane

"Thank you so much for letting us in," I said to Dominic's mom as we waited for her to unlock the door. I didn't want to risk him waking Olivia up to come let us in, and thankfully my mom had given me his mom's phone number. It was convenient that he lived next door to his parents, so she didn't have to go far.

"Not a problem," she replied with a wink.

"You guys need to be quiet, okay? Go inside, take your shoes off, and find somewhere to sit down. Olivia is sick, and we need her to rest." I looked at Mikey and Sally, making sure they both understood before we went inside.

Abby and Nate were on their way, so I texted her to let her know the door was unlocked and that they could come in when they got there. I set down the container of applesauce I'd brought for Olivia and tiptoed into the living room, where I found Dominic asleep on the couch with Olivia snuggled into his chest, his arms wrapped protectively around her.

I wasn't sure how long he'd been asleep, but I hated the thought of waking him up. They looked so peaceful together and my heart ached at the thought of what he would look like with *our baby*. I immediately scolded myself for going there and reminded myself that I didn't even know for sure whether I was pregnant.

The kids quietly walked into the living room and sat down on the loveseat across from him while I sat in the recliner. It looked old but comfortable and worn, so I hadn't expected it to creak so loudly when I sat down.

Dominic's eyes flung open as he looked around, startled.

Once he noticed me, his shoulders relaxed, and I saw the ghost of a smile on his lips.

"Hey," he whispered.

"Hi."

He looked at the kids and smiled warmly at them. At that time, Olivia started to fuss and shift position on his chest. He lifted his hand and touched her forehead and then frowned.

"Fever?" I whispered, more so mouthing the word than saying it.

He nodded. She lifted her head and looked around, then started crying and pulling at her ear. I stood up, walked over to them, and reached out to take her.

"Here, let me help."

He lifted her to me and then I stepped back so he could get up. She was awake but curled her head into my chest and tried to get comfortable.

"I'm sorry you don't feel well," I said softly, caressing her back. "When was the last time she had Tylenol?"

He picked up his phone and checked the time.

"About six hours ago. She was sleeping, so I didn't want to wake her up to give it to her."

"That's fine," I assured him. "It's better for her to sleep when she can."

He stood up and stretched, his arms lifting above his head and pulling his t-shirt up his toned abs. I looked away, hoping no one could see the blush creeping up my cheeks.

"I'll go get some."

I nodded and bounced her gently as she started to fuss.

"I brought her some applesauce," I said, following him into the adjoining kitchen. "I wasn't sure if she'd eat it, but I thought we could try."

"That sounds perfect, thank you." He tilted the bottle and pulled the plunger of the syringe to draw the Tylenol.

"Abby and Nate should be here soon with dinner," I added, suddenly feeling nervous around him. "Sorry for intruding on you; we just wanted to help."

"It's alright. I appreciate it." He smiled and then stood right in front of me, our bodies almost touching as he lifted the syringe to Olivia's mouth and waited for her to take the medicine.

Once she was done, he tossed the syringe into the sink and wrote down the time he'd given it to her on a notepad that had a list of the times before. I was impressed that he was being so diligent in making sure he knew when he'd given her medicine. A lot of parents I worked with—especially fathers—didn't bother doing that.

Olivia shifted in my arms again and seemed to be getting uncomfortable.

"Do you want to see if she'll take some food?" I asked, knowing she was likely getting hungry since she'd been asleep for so long.

"Yeah, that sounds great. Her highchair is over in the corner. If you can grab that, I'll turn something on the TV for Mikey and Sally."

"Perfect."

I hated the way butterflies floated through my stomach every time he thought about my kids without having to be asked. He was constantly considerate of them and went out of his way to make sure they were included in everything that was going on.

I grabbed the highchair from the corner, brought it to the round kitchen table, and then sat her in it. I ensured she was strapped in and secure before grabbing the applesauce from the counter. Dominic was in the living room, scrolling through the guide on the TV while asking the kids what they wanted to watch.

A few minutes later, Abby and Nate showed up, letting themselves in. We all gathered around the table and ate while I focused on Olivia and the strange pull in my heart that I felt for her.

Everyone was talking and laughter filled the room, which was nice. I was glad that even though I didn't want to do anything tonight, it had worked out anyway. This was much better than sitting at home, worrying about whether or not I was pregnant. Before I left work, I'd scheduled an appointment with Doctor Nicoli and was able to get in on Friday. He'd requested the blood work in advance, which I'd done as soon as I could today.

"So, what do you think?" Abby asked, watching me as if she knew the thoughts that were racing through my mind.

"I'm sorry. About what?"

"You weren't listening at all, were you?"

"I was focused on feeding Olivia," I said, giving her a look.

"Is that why she's holding the spoon and there's a puddle of applesauce on the highchair?" she asked with a smirk.

I looked down and found Olivia smiling up at me as she shook the spoon in the air.

"You're a quick one, aren't you?" I laughed, bopping her gently on the nose.

Penny laughed from the other side of the table as she sat on Nate's lap, chewing on a French fry.

"Are you guys plotting against me?" I teased, smiling at Penny. "Do you want what she has?"

Olivia dropped her spoon, then opened and closed her fingers as she tried to reach for the fry. I laughed and looked at Dominic, who was already gathering food from his plate to give to Olivia. I grabbed some napkins and cleaned up the mess on her tray so he could put the new food down.

I pushed the applesauce to the side and sighed as she chowed down on the good stuff in front of her.

"I don't blame you; I'm a sucker for Surf 'N Shack too." I winked and she giggled more.

"I feel like you're trying to avoid me," Abby teased, drawing my attention back to her.

"Not at all. I was just distracted for a moment. Tell me again; I'm all ears."

"I was saying that you and I need a girl's trip this weekend. Nate will watch Penny, and I've already talked to mom and dad. They're on board with taking Mikey and Sally. So, what do you say?"

"A girl's trip? For what?" I was genuinely confused because Abby and I hadn't taken a girl's trip together since before I had the kids.

"To get away. Reset. Relax. Focus on the future and what we want from it."

"Oh," I stammered, not sure what to say.

"I've got everything planned already. All you have to do is be ready to go at 8 am Saturday."

I looked at Mikey and Sally, curious to see what they thought about this.

"Are you guys okay if I go?" I asked, feeling everyone's eyes on me.

"Yeah, you should go, Mom. We always have fun at Grandma and Grandpa's." Mikey smiled across the table at me as he sat beside Dominic, who was studying me intently.

"I'm going to ask them if we can do another movie night!" Sally clapped her hands excitedly. "We can order a pizza and stay up late eating candy and popcorn!"

My eyes widened, knowing how hyper they would be from that.

"Don't worry, you won't be there to deal with it," Abby whispered loudly behind her hand.

We all laughed, and I felt some of the tension in my shoulders dissipate.

"Okay, sure," I sighed. "I'm in."

After everyone was done eating, Abby and I cleaned up the kitchen and sent the guys and kids to the living room so Dominic could rest with Olivia, who was getting fussy again. We'd used paper plates so there would be minimal clean up, but there were still cups to wash, plus random dishes that Dominic hadn't had a chance to get into the dishwasher with Olivia being sick and needing him to hold her.

I scrubbed the sippy cups and set them on the rack to dry, then washed the Tylenol syringes so they were clean when he needed them again.

Abby loaded the last few dishes into the dishwasher, then closed it and looked at me.

"So," I said slowly. "What's this girl's trip really about?"

She looked into the living room and then back at me.

"Well, given that I've taken pregnancy tests every day since Sunday, and they've all been negative, I thought you could use a few days away to process the news."

I swallowed hard, looking down at the floor.

"I don't know what you're talking about."

"Jane, two of the tests were positive, and they weren't mine."

"Maybe they were a false positive," I objected, though we both knew I was lying through my teeth.

"Really, Jane?" She planted her hand on her hip and pinned me with a look.

I rolled my eyes and exhaled heavily.

"Fine," I sighed. "They weren't false."

"Have you taken more?"

I nodded.

"And?"

I looked into the living room, watching Dominic cuddle Olivia to his chest as she tried to fall asleep. He laughed at something Nate said, his dimples making him even more attractive.

"And," I exhaled. "I think I'm pregnant."

Twenty-Five
Dominic

"I fold," I muttered, tossing my cards down on the table. It was Saturday night, and Nate had invited me over for a poker night while Abby and Jane were out of town. Abby's parents had asked to take Penny since they were having Mike and Sally sleepover, and then my parents found out and begged to have a sleepover with Olivia. Apparently, all of the grandparents had gotten together at Doug and Rhonda's house where they had a pizza and movie night with the kids and I was honored that they all wanted to include my daughter.

"Me too," Jones said.

It was Capshaw and Nate left in the game, which ended like all of the other rounds before. I sat back and sipped my beer while they finished. Capshaw won again, and we all laughed at how frustrated Nate was that he couldn't beat him.

"What can I say? I'm good at cards," Capshaw laughed.

"Well, maybe you could use that talent and find a woman," Nate teased.

Capshaw held a hand to his heart and pretended to be wounded by his words.

"Not all of us can be as lucky as you and fall in love with our best friend." Capshaw lifted his beer to his lips and took a drink.

"Well, you could. But first, you'd have to be friends with someone. Maybe stop scaring them away. You guys want more wings?" Nate got up and grabbed the empty beer bottles as he headed to the kitchen.

"Sure," we all said at slightly different times and then laughed.

It felt different to hang out with just the guys and not have to worry about anything else. While I missed seeing Jane and being around her, I also really liked the vibe with the guys and felt like maybe I was finally starting to fit in. Capshaw was around the same age as me, only a few years older. Jones was the baby of the group, which made him an easy target for them to pick on him. But it was all in good fun, and he gave it right back to them with the random *gramps* jokes aimed more so at Nate.

A few minutes later, Nate returned with a plate piled high with wings, some ranch dressing, and a handful of beers tucked into his arm.

"Thanks for the invite tonight," I said, accepting one of the beers he offered me.

"Not a problem. We try to do this more often, but things have been busier with Penny, so it's more sporadic than it used to be."

We all loaded our plates with food while Nate shuffled the deck of cards. I knew what he meant, my life had changed drastically after having Olivia, and now I didn't have the same free time I used to. Not that I was complaining—I loved my daughter dearly and would gladly give all of that up, but it was still nice to have tonight with the guys.

"Alright, now who's going to kick Capshaw's ass in the next round?" Nate asked as he dealt another round.

"You can try, but no one can take me down." Capshaw smiled smugly.

"Just wait until you meet the right woman," Nate said. "They'll take you down and you won't ever get up again."

The poker night wrapped up around eleven, and I headed home. I was tired and wanted to get some sleep, but it felt weird not having Olivia there to take care of. Thankfully, her ear infection had gotten better, and she didn't end up needing any antibiotics for it. It had been a long few days while I waited for her to get better, but Jane had made sure to keep in touch and make sure we didn't need anything.

Things between us still felt odd, and I couldn't shake the feeling that something was wrong. I hated that she wouldn't talk to me about whatever it was, but I hated even more that it reminded me too much of Rebecca and how she used to hide things from me. It had been one of the things that first divided us, especially when I found out she had been using drugs.

Rebecca and I had been together for over five years before the world came crashing down on me the first time I found her unconscious on the couch from an overdose. When she'd come to, at the hospital, she'd promised me that it was a one-time thing and that she'd learned her lesson. Foolishly, I believed her.

I later discovered that it hadn't been the first time, nor would it be the last. I tried everything I could to get her clean, but nothing was stronger than the drugs she craved. We went to therapy, and she did rehab for six months. I even gave her an ultimatum. But then one day, she came home crying that she thought she was pregnant and didn't know what to do.

We sat down and talked, and for once, I felt like I was getting through to her. She agreed to stay clean during the pregnancy, but I was skeptical, given her track record. Once she reached the halfway mark and the baby looked healthy on the ultrasounds, I stupidly asked her to marry me. She said yes but didn't want a big wedding, so we went to the courthouse and got married through the Justice of the Peace.

After Olivia was born, Rebecca left, and we didn't see her again other than a few times when she'd shown up to ask for money to buy more drugs. I'd filed for divorce and paid a private investigator to track her down so she could be served. I was worried that a judge would dismiss our paperwork if they knew she was high and didn't know what she was signing. Surprisingly, she signed and the divorce was granted, so I didn't question it. Maybe it was a sign from the universe that I was supposed to be free from her so that I could move on and raise the daughter she didn't want.

I laid down in bed, staring at the wall as I remembered the way I felt when I packed us up and made the move to start over in Beaumont Creek. It was an amazing feeling, similar to what I felt whenever I was around Jane.

Twenty-Six
Jane

Abby and I had pampered ourselves the entire day. She'd booked us a room at a fancy hotel in Ocean City, and we'd spent the day at the indoor pool eating snacks and drinking fruity virgin cocktails. By dinner, we'd gone back to the room with the intention of cleaning up and heading down to the steakhouse that everyone raved about, but we were both too exhausted to go.

Instead, we'd ordered room service and ate dinner on our beds, in our pajamas. It was exactly what I needed. Well, that and the molten lava cake we both decided to indulge in. My stomach was beyond full while my mind still raced with everything that had happened this week.

Yesterday, I had my appointment with Doctor Nicoli, and it was confirmed through the bloodwork that I was pregnant. It was still so early that it made sense why a few of the tests had a hard time showing the line. I scheduled an appointment for my first ultrasound in three weeks and still needed to talk to Dominic.

"Do you want to watch another food show, or should we switch to a true crime one instead?" Abby asked, flipping through the channels.

"I can't stand the thought of any more food," I laughed, rubbing my stomach, which felt like it was going to explode. "But, I don't think I want to watch true crime right before I go to sleep, so what other options do we have?"

"Don't be starving my niece or nephew; they need food," Abby scolded, giving me a genuine smile before turning her attention back to the TV, looking for something else for us to watch. "How about Friends? You can be like Joey, who doesn't share food."

"I told you if you wanted some nachos, to get them before they were gone." I laughed.

"There wasn't a chance to unless I wanted to lose a finger."

"I was hungry." I shrugged.

"I'm just glad that you're eating. Usually, when you get stressed, you *stop* eating, and I don't want you starving my future best friend."

"Hey," I pulled my head back in surprise. "I thought *I* was your best friend. And Nate. And Penny!"

"I have many best friends, including you, Nate, and Penny. You can't forget Mikey and Sally, too."

I smiled, loving how much she loved my kids.

"How am I going to tell them?" I asked, feeling my throat tighten with emotion.

"You'll find a way. But I think you should talk to Dominic first. Maybe you guys can come up with a way to talk to them together?"

"They don't even know that we were seeing each other. Can we call it that? Do I tell them that he was a one-night stand? How do I even define this thing between us?"

"Slow down," Abby said calmly. "You don't have to have the answer to everything right now. And honestly, I don't think this was a one-night stand for Dominic. He's been interested in you from the start, but you're the one who's always kept him an arm's length away. I think if you guys decide to talk to the kids together, maybe you start with that you guys are dating and then ease them into the baby news."

"Maybe I don't tell them until I've made it through the first trimester? I'm only five weeks; it's still so early. If something happened…."

"Nothing is going to happen, but I understand wanting to wait. This is big news for all of you and shouldn't be taken lightly. Just take it one step at a time. It'll be okay."

I nodded and exhaled slowly, trying to keep my blood pressure from rising again.

"Oh, this is my favorite part!" Abby said, pointing the remote toward the TV to turn it up.

I leaned against the pile of pillows behind me and watched as Rachel and Ross kissed on the floor of the auditorium and remembered how it felt to kiss Dominic the first time. It was different, and there was this pull to him that made me feel closer to him than anyone else I'd ever been with in my life.

We watched TV for an hour, Abby laughing at the corny jokes and innuendos while I thought about Dominic and wondered what he was up to tonight. I wanted to text him but it felt weird to reach out to him and pretend like I wasn't keeping this huge secret. No matter how hard I tried, I couldn't erase the image of him at the supermarket when he spotted the pregnancy tests. I knew that he was suspicious that they were mine and I regretted not just telling him right then and there.

I would have, but I was so worried about how he would react. Would he be like Rick, who acted like he was excited about it, though he wasn't? I knew that Rick didn't necessarily care either way about becoming a father, but I'd hoped that after we got married, he would change his mind and want it. That it would be the next logical step for us to take since he knew how badly I wanted to have a family. But when I'd curled up on his lap and handed him the gift bag with the pregnancy tests inside, there was a look of panic on his face that he quickly tried to disguise with shock.

I'd been trying to rid myself of the feelings Rick imposed on me during our marriage, but it was hard. You couldn't just walk away from someone you had vowed to spend the rest of your life with and then pretend that you weren't impacted by the things that had transpired during your time with them.

But I had to remind myself that Dominic wasn't Rick. He wasn't like any of the guys I'd dated after him, either. Even Capshaw was better than Rick, and even though he was only a few years older than Dominic, they still weren't the same either.

Capshaw was more immature, though he was fun in the bedroom. But he lacked the basic relationship skills that I wanted, and that meant that there wasn't a future for us. Not only that, he didn't have the same connection with my kids that Dominic did. While I understood that it was hard to step into a relationship with someone who already has kids, there was a huge difference between Dominic and Capshaw in how they interacted with Mikey and Sally.

With Capshaw, it always felt like it was forced and uncomfortable for him. I couldn't imagine leaving him alone to watch them like I did the other day with Dominic when I had to go to work. Dominic acted like he enjoyed hanging out with them, but not only that, he seemed to respect them the same way they respected him. It was completely different, but I loved the way we were when we all hung out, and it felt like we could actually be a family.

And now, thanks to a broken condom and failed birth control, we were going to be one.

I reached over, grabbed my phone from the bed beside me, and scrolled until I found the text message thread I had going with Dominic.

Me: Hey, would you like to have dinner this week? Just the two of us?

I chewed my nail anxiously as I waited for him to respond. I could easily ask my parents or Abby to watch the kids for me so I could go, but I didn't want to make things complicated for him by asking his parents to watch Olivia. Even though I knew they helped out often, I didn't want to assume anything.

Dominic: I would love to take you to dinner. When would you like to go?

Me: I'm free whenever. We'll be back in town tomorrow afternoon, not that we have to go tomorrow night.

Dominic: Tomorrow night works for me. What time can I pick you up?

Me: I can be ready by seven.

Dominic: Sounds great. Let me know where you'd like to go and I'll see you tomorrow night.

Me: Okay, thank you.

I inhaled deeply and slowly released the breath. We were

one step closer to me telling him and not having to keep this secret any longer. I ignored the curious glances coming from Abby and pretended to focus on the TV.

My phone vibrated with another text message alert.

Dominic: I can't wait to see you. I've missed you.

My heart fluttered wildly in my chest as I grinned like a fool.

Twenty- Seven
Dominic

I looked in the mirror one last time before I grabbed my car keys and phone from the table and headed out the door to pick Jane up. My parents were watching Olivia for me and couldn't stop smiling when I told them that I was taking Jane out to dinner. Hell—I couldn't believe it myself.

I'd made reservations at 727, an upscale oceanfront restaurant Nate said Jane loved after I asked him for suggestions when she couldn't decide where to go. The dress code wasn't strict, but I'd gone with a pair of dress slacks and a buttoned-down shirt just to make sure I wasn't too casual.

When I got to Jane's house, she was standing at the front door, wearing a tight-fitting black dress that stopped mid-thigh. I swallowed hard as I pulled into the driveway, desperate to touch her and slide my hands up her legs to see whether she was wearing any panties or not. From where I was sitting, I would bet money that she wasn't, given that I couldn't see any panty lines.

She looked up and smiled when she heard me pull up. I parked the car and got out to open the passenger door for her.

"Hey," she said, reaching in to hug me as my hands wrapped around her waist.

"Hi. You look incredible."

"Thank you. I've had this dress for a while but have never had an excuse to wear it until tonight."

I smiled as I reached over and pulled the door open.

"I hope you weren't waiting long," I said as she climbed inside.

"No, not at all. My parents just picked the kids up a few minutes ago and I came to walk them out."

I closed the door as she buckled up, then took a steadying breath before I got in. It'd been a while since I'd been alone with Jane, and I was worried that I wasn't going to be able to control myself and fight the desire I had to reach over and kiss her.

Once we arrived at the restaurant, I escorted her inside and followed as the hostess showed us to the booth in the back. It was incredibly private and sat beside the full-length window overlooking the ocean. The view was incredible, but nothing compared to Jane.

She smoothed her dress and slid in while I sat on the other side. It was quiet, with dim lighting and soft music floating through the air, setting the atmosphere for us to enjoy a romantic dinner together.

"May I start you with something to drink besides water?" The waiter asked as soon as the hostess walked off.

"Would you like wine?" I asked Jane.

"I'm okay with water for now, thank you."

I noticed a faint reddish tint to her skin and smiled at the waiter so he got the message to leave and give us some space.

We looked over the menu quietly, though I already knew

what I wanted. Not that Jane was on tonight's list of specialties, but that didn't mean I didn't want to devour her.

"Do you know what you're getting?" I asked, my eyes scrolling down the list of seafood options.

"I'm pregnant," she answered, blurting the words out.

I lowered my menu to the table and stared at her.

She was still holding hers and started to raise it slightly to cover her face when I reached over and brought her hand down.

"You're pregnant," I repeated, the words finally processing in my head.

Jane's eyes studied me cautiously as if she expected me to bolt and run out the door.

She nodded and then finally let her menu fall onto the table with mine.

"Okay," I said slowly, unsure of how to respond. While I had expected this, I was still somehow unprepared to hear her say it.

"I'm about five weeks."

"It's yours."

"I know I said I was on birth control, and I am. I'm sorry, I don't know why it didn't work. I don't ever miss one, and I've been on it for over—"

"Jane," I said sternly, stopping her from the rambling she'd started. "You're pregnant with my baby."

She nodded, and I noticed tears starting to build in her

beautiful brown eyes. Her hands trembled slightly as she reached for the napkin on her lap and tried to wipe them away as she turned her head to look out the window.

I got up and slid into the other side of the booth next to her.

"You're having my baby?" I asked with a cheesy smile. I wrapped one arm around her shoulders and pulled her to me as the other slid across her stomach and rubbed the spot where my child was growing inside her.

"I am," she sobbed, desperately trying to wipe her tears away.

"Baby, why are you crying?"

"Because I didn't know how you would take the news. It wasn't like we were trying to have a baby. We only had sex once, and now I'm pregnant. We're not even dating," she said shakily.

"Okay, so let's fix that."

"Fix what?" she asked, finally turning to face me.

"The part about us not dating. Let's date." I shrugged.

She rolled her eyes, and a faint smile flashed across her face.

"You don't have to do that, Dominic. I don't expect you to."

"I know I don't. I want to. Jane, will you be my girlfriend and incredibly sexy baby mama?"

She tilted her head back and laughed out loud. It was the most glorious sound I'd ever heard, aside from the ones Olivia made.

"Say yes, please," I begged while tickling her sides and pulling her closer. "I can't get enough of you, and it seems we're destined to be together anyway. So say you'll be mine."

"Okay, I'll be yours," she laughed. "I mean, you did knock me up and brought me to a beautiful restaurant for dinner."

"And, if we have time when we're done, I'll take you home for dessert," I whispered in her ear. "Though I don't know if I can wait that long with you sitting beside me wearing that dress."

My hand slid down her waist and rested on her thigh, teasing the spot where the fabric ended. I wanted to touch and tease her but didn't want to do anything she didn't want me to. But then she started to spread her thighs for me and I saw the way her eyes darkened when she looked at me.

The tablecloth was long enough to hide what we were doing under the table, and it helped that we were in the corner of the restaurant with no one else seated beside us. I leaned over and kissed her, feeling the warmth of her mouth as she parted it and allowed my tongue to swipe over hers.

She moaned softly into the kiss as my hand slid higher, pushing her dress up until I could touch her pussy. Just like I'd guessed, she wasn't wearing any panties underneath, which made me instantly hard. I wanted to bend her over the table and fuck her right then and there but couldn't. But that didn't mean that I couldn't make her come at the table.

I slipped a finger along her slit, loving the way she hissed between her teeth as she opened her legs further for me.

"You're such a good girl," I coaxed. "Spread those legs for me, baby. Let me play with that sweet pussy and make her come."

"I'm so horny right now," she confessed, her eyes pinched closed as I pushed a finger inside her.

"I'm horny for you all the time, Jane. I can't tell you how many times I've jerked off to thoughts of you while in the shower or late at night when I couldn't sleep. I picture your mouth wrapped tightly around my cock as you suck me off. I think about watching your pussy as you ride me again in front of the mirror. You make me so fucking hard, Jane." I reached down with my free hand and guided it to my cock to show her just how much she turned me on.

She whimpered quietly and I slipped another finger in, pumping both in and out of her.

"Have you decided what you'd like this evening?" the waiter asked as he returned, standing only a few feet away from where I was fingering my *girlfriend.* It felt freaking incredible to call her that.

"Did you know what you wanted, sweetheart?" I asked, watching how she desperately tried to focus on him instead of what my fingers were doing to her. I didn't bother to pull them out when I felt how wet she got once she noticed he was there.

"I'll, um, do the chicken." Her voice was strained as she answered, but he didn't question her as he wrote it down on his notepad and then looked at me.

"I'll have the surf and turf, please."

"Anything else?"

"No, thank you," I answered, brushing her clit with my thumb.

She grabbed my cock in return, squeezing hard as she tried not to make any noise as the waiter cleared the wine glasses from the table.

After he was gone, I leaned in and kissed the spot right

below her ear while my fingers continued to play with her.

"You feel so good," I whispered. "I can't wait to be inside of you again."

"I want it too. I'm so close."

"I want you to come for me, baby, but not yet."

She looked up at me with the saddest look and I had to bite the inside of my cheek to keep from laughing.

"Don't worry, you will soon. But I want to play for a few more minutes."

The hostess passed by and led another couple to a table across from us. I took the opportunity to pump faster, pleased by the noises I could hear from how wet she was.

"Looks like we might have an audience," I said. "Do you think you can be quiet while you come, or should we invite them to join us? Maybe they want to watch as your pussy spasms around my finger, desperate for my cock next."

She chewed her lower lip as she looked past me at the couple who was around our age. The woman wore a dress slightly shorter than Jane's and the man appeared to appreciate it as much as I did.

The tablecloth was long enough to hide what they were doing, but the way he shifted in his seat made me think that maybe he was about to do the same thing I was doing.

"Maybe they'll give us a show, too," I said quietly, watching as the woman scooted her chair closer to his. We could see their feet, but that was it.

Suddenly, her heels went from being crossed at the ankles

to spread apart as she held the menu in front of her face and appeared to be studying it.

"I bet he's slipping his finger inside of her right now, too. She probably didn't wear any panties, just like someone else that I know."

"Mmmmm," Jane panted, her eyes still fixated on the couple across from us.

"Do you want to come before her or with her?" I asked, rubbing her clit with my thumb.

"I want to come now," she panted. "I'm so ready, Dominic. Make me come, please."

I leaned over, ignoring the other couple as I kissed her neck and fucked her harder with my fingers. I continued to rub her clit until I felt her walls tighten around me. She exhaled sharply and gripped the tablecloth as she came, her breathing loud and erratic.

A few seconds later, she was done and her eyes fluttered open. I kissed her lips and pulled my fingers out, desperately wanting to lick them clean so I could taste her.

"Better?" I asked quietly.

She nodded and smiled at me.

"Looks like they had other plans after all," I joked, letting out a soft chuckle.

The woman was no longer sitting at the table, but the tablecloth was short enough to show her heels as she kneeled beneath the table and gave him head. He leaned back in the chair, setting his menu down as his hand dipped beneath the table. We watched as discreetly as we could as his mouth pulled tightly into a thin line as he tried to contain his moan while he came in her mouth.

"Do you think they'll let us take our order to go?" Jane asked, rubbing her hand over my still achingly hard erection.

Twenty- Eight

Jane

"Are you sure you're really okay with all of this?" I asked as I held Dominic's hand while we walked out to his truck. We decided to go ahead and enjoy dinner at the restaurant, but we still hurried so we could also go home for a quick round of *dessert* before we had to pick up the kids.

"Of course," he replied, squeezing my hand gently. "Why wouldn't I be?"

I shrugged.

"I don't know. Because it wasn't something we ever talked about, nor did we plan it."

"True, but either way, it's happening, and I would rather embrace it than freak out about it."

I stopped walking and turned to look at him, wrapping my arms around myself to ward off the chill that was spreading across my skin.

"It's okay to be freaked out. Heck, I've done that a handful of times already," I laughed. "This is a big, life-changing thing happening to us. I wouldn't judge you if you freaked out too."

He grinned his dimpled smile and pulled me into his arms, rubbing them gently to warm me up.

"I promise, Jane, I'm not going to freak out."

"Well, that makes one of us." My words were partly muffled by my mouth being pressed up against his chest, but his chuckle made me think he heard me.

"It's going to be alright. You'll see."

I pulled back slightly and tilted my head to see him better.

"How are you so confident about all of this?"

"I just know in my heart that it will be. I know it might be too soon to say it, but I can't help how I feel, Jane. I love you. More than I could ever put into words, but I do. I love you. I love Mikey, Sally, and Olivia. And I already love the little peanut growing inside of you."

"You're so cute," I said, feeling like my heart was going to burst with happiness. "I love you too, Dominic."

He leaned in and kissed the tip of my nose.

"Why don't we go home, and I can show you how much I love you."

I giggled and let him lead me across the parking lot before helping me into his truck. I tucked my dress underneath me and then buckled up while he climbed inside.

He turned the key to start the engine when my phone dinged with a text message. I pulled it out and frowned when I saw a message from my mother asking how much longer I would be. Apparently, Sally was getting tired and wanted to go to bed, so my mom wasn't sure whether to keep them overnight or if I would be coming for them soon.

I replied, letting her know I would be there in thirty

minutes, forty-five tops. I shoved my phone into the black satin clutch and set it on my lap.

"Everything alright?" Dominic asked, noticing the change in my mood.

"Yeah, Sally wants to go home, so I need to go pick them up. I'm sorry to cut the night short for us."

"Don't worry about that at all. Our children will always come first, Jane."

He reached over the console and held my hand, making me feel like everything was going to be okay.

We were almost to my house when an idea hit me.

"Hey, pull over on that street," I said, pointing in the direction I wanted him to go.

"Okay."

He did as I asked and followed the road to where it dead-ended next to the park. There weren't any street lights over on this side, so if anyone were around, they'd be on the opposite where the parking lot was fully lit.

I unbuckled my seatbelt and waited for him to turn off the engine.

"We don't have much time," I breathed as I quickly swiveled my legs over the console and straddled his lap. I lifted my dress, pulling it up around my waist as his eyes traveled down my body to my bare pussy.

"You don't get to wear panties ever again," he murmured before undoing his button and pulling down his zipper. "I want to eat that pretty little pussy so bad, but for now, I'm going to sit back and let her milk my cock."

I chewed my lower lip and waited for him to pull his dick out. He gripped it tightly in his hand and my mouth watered at how big and hard it was. I wanted to do so much more than we had time for tonight, but this was going to have to do for now.

"Ready?" I asked, still staring at the one-eyed beast instead of the handsome devil it was attached to.

He moaned as he lowered my hips on top of his cock and I sank down, taking him as deep inside of me as possible.

"Fuck," he groaned, closing his eyes and resting his head against the headrest.

"Mmm hmmm," I agreed, grinding down on him as he leaned forward and tried to free one of my nipples from the plunging neckline of the dress.

I leaned back, making it easier for him as I bounced up and down, loving every second of it.

"You feel so fucking good, Jane. Last time was amazing, but being inside of you without any protection is a whole other level of ecstasy."

"Yes," I cried out, partly agreeing with him while also feeling myself climb toward a mind-blowing orgasm.

I shifted my position slightly, rubbing my clit against his cock as I moaned. I didn't wait for permission before using him for my pleasure, pounding down on him hard and fast as I sought my release. Seconds later, I felt the first spasm as I clenched around him and came hard on his dick. His fingers dug deeper into my hips, holding me in place as I squeezed him while he came inside me.

We were both breathless as I leaned forward and rested my forehead on his.

"That was incredible," he breathed. "I can't wait to do that again."

"Same," I sighed.

"Not to rush a good thing, but I better get you home so you can pick up the kids."

I nodded and groaned quietly as I slipped off him and sat in the passenger seat again. My body was more relaxed than it had been a few minutes ago, but I already missed the fullness of having him inside me.

He reached into the glove box and pulled out a box of tissues, handing them to me to grab a few before cleaning himself up. It felt like we were being naughty teenagers who were sneaking around having sex so our parents couldn't catch us, and the thought made me giggle.

"What's so funny?" Dominic asked, grinning along with me.

"Nothing," I said with a laugh. "I was just thinking about how happy I am."

And for once, I wasn't lying.

Twenty-Nine
Dominic

It was a long three weeks of not being able to tell anyone that Jane was pregnant. I understood her concern about sharing the news before we had our first ultrasound, but the excitement in me was overwhelming, and I felt like I needed to tell someone. So far, the only person besides Jane and me who knew was Abby, and Jane assured me that meant that Nate knew as well because Abby couldn't keep a secret to save her life.

"Are you nervous?" I asked Jane, holding her hand as we sat in the waiting room.

"A little bit. You?"

"Maybe just a little. More excited to see our baby, though."

She pressed her lips into a thin line, and I knew she was holding back the fears she wanted to say. *What if something happened. What if there is no baby? I'm forty-two years old, and it might be harder for my body to carry this pregnancy. What if the tests were all false positives? What if they mixed my blood work up with someone else's?*

I only knew those were the likely things going through her mind because she had slipped and mentioned them to me a few times when we talked after the kids had gone to bed. She was tired and I'd found that meant that she was more relaxed and open with what she was thinking.

"Jane?" An older woman with curly gray hair stood at the door to the back offices, holding a clipboard to her chest as she waited for us.

"Good morning. We'll be in room 3." She held the door open before leading us down the hallway and stepping aside for us to enter. "Doctor Nicoli will be in to do your ultrasound in a few minutes. Please remove any clothing from the waist down and cover yourself with this sheet. I'll step out to give you some privacy."

Jane nodded and started to undress as soon as the nurse left the room. I looked away and studied the large canvas pictures of newborn babies. Unlike most men, it didn't freak me out or make me want to run in the other direction. Instead, I felt the comfort and excitement I felt every time I thought about Jane having my baby.

I heard the paper on the table rustle as she climbed up and got situated. I stood beside her, kissing her head while holding her close. We didn't say anything; we just took the time to be connected to each other before our first ultrasound.

A few minutes later, there was a knock on the door before the doctor walked in.

"Good morning, Jane," he said, extending his hand to her. "Dominic, it's a pleasure to meet you."

I shook the hand he offered me, already feeling more at ease with how nice he was.

"Good morning, Doctor Nicoli," Jane replied.

"Nice to meet you too," I answered, stepping away from Jane and shoving my hands into my pockets to keep from reaching for her.

"Shall we get started?" he asked, pulling the stool from under the counter and sitting down.

Suddenly my heart started racing, and the easiness I felt before was quickly replaced with nerves as I watched him slide what looked like a condom over this wand-looking thing that I guessed was used for the ultrasound. I didn't get to go with Rebecca to her first ultrasound because of work, so I was only there for the ones they did on her stomach.

In an effort to be prepared for today, I'd taken the time to research what to expect during this visit and knew that they would have to go in vaginally to get the image because of how small the baby was. Even still, I felt the color drain from my face as he talked to Jane about the weather while he slid it inside her—a place only I was supposed to be— and then studied the screen to locate the baby.

I sat down, not wanting to embarrass myself by fainting. I wasn't a fainter, but sometimes things changed, and this felt like the right situation for that to happen.

He leaned closer to the screen and moved the wand around until he found whatever he was looking for.

"There you go," he said happily, pointing to a spot on the monitor with his other hand. "There's your baby. It looks like you're right around eight weeks. The heartbeat looks nice and strong. Do you want to hear it?"

"Yes, please," Jane said, her voice thick with emotion.

I stood beside her and rested my hand on her shoulder as we both waited. A few seconds later, a fast, thumping noise filled the room, and we grinned at each other while we listened to it.

It sounded a little different than I remembered from hearing Olivia's heartbeat during the few ultrasounds Rebecca had with her that I got to go to, but then again, that was over a year ago.

"Is everything okay?" Jane asked, noticing Doctor Nicoli staring at the screen while he moved the wand around.

He stopped again, this time his eyebrows rising on his forehead before he started smiling again.

"There you are, I was wondering where you were hiding," he said quietly, more so to himself than us.

"Who's hiding where?" I asked, leaning forward slightly to get a better view.

Suddenly the screen changed as he moved the wand again, and this time, there were two spots that he was pointing to.

"Here's baby A, and right here is baby B."

I wish I could say I knew how Jane handled the news, but the floor greeted me as I landed on it with a loud thump instead. Apparently, twins were the one thing that could make me pass out after all.

Thirty

Jane

I sat in the office chair, waiting for Dominic to finish drinking the ice water Doctor Nicoli brought him. He'd stepped out to give us some privacy after Dominic woke up a few moments after passing out. While I'd been shocked to find out that we were having twins, I hadn't expected Dominic's reaction.

"Are you okay?" I asked cautiously, my hands folded in my lap.

"Mmm hmm." He lifted the paper cup and took another drink.

I rubbed my lips together, not knowing what to say.

"It's okay to freak out."

"I'm not freaked out," he objected, though we both knew it was a lie.

There was a knock on the door and Doctor Nicoli came back in.

"You feeling any better?" he asked Dominic as he sat down on the stool again.

"I'm okay," he said, nodding and drinking the rest of the water in his cup.

Doctor Nicoli extended his hand to take his trash and tossed it in the bin next to the table.

"I know this can be a lot to take in at once. Twins are fairly common with geriatric pregnancies, and Jane is healthy, so I'm not worried—"

"We only had sex once," Dominic blurted out, surprising both myself and Doctor Nicoli.

"Well, sometimes that's all it takes," Doctor Nicoli said, smiling at us.

"No, we had sex once, so there should only be one baby. Not two. We only did it once."

I covered my mouth with my hand to keep from laughing but freaked out Dominic was adorable, and I couldn't help but love him even more right now.

"Um," Doctor Nicoli hesitated for a moment. "That's not really how it works with twins. Regardless of how many times you have sex, you can still conceive multiple babies from one *encounter.* In this case, it looks like two of your sperm were both able to fertilize two separate egg, which is how you guys conceived fraternal twins."

"Fuckin super swimmers," Dominic muttered, scrubbing a hand down his face. "They were probably conspiring against me and chewed a hole through the damn condom. That's why it broke."

I tried to pull a calming breath through my nose and slowly tried to exhale it so I wouldn't laugh.

Doctor Nicoli was about to respond but looked at me first. I shook my head, letting him know that he didn't need to discuss the strength of sperm or their latex-chewing abilities. I would get Dominic out of here and take him somewhere where he could have whatever kind of freak-out he needed.

"Do you guys have any questions for me?" he asked, looking between us.

"I think we're good," I replied, surprisingly calm though the nervous laughter was still sitting right at the surface.

"I have a question," Dominic said, raising his hand like a kid in class.

Doctor Nicoli nodded and waited for him to ask it.

"Should I keep using condoms when we have sex? I don't want to keep knocking her up since my guys seem to be so aggressive."

I turned my head but not before the laughter erupted. I could feel their eyes on me and hated that I might have been making things worse for Dominic. I didn't want him to think I was laughing at him, even though I technically was. He was adorable, and I loved how concerned he was not to knock me up again right now.

"You're good," Doctor Nicoli assured him. "If it makes you feel better to use a condom, that's up to you. There's no harm in it for the mother or the babies. But I can assure you, the chances of Jane having another egg fertilized while pregnant is incredibly low and not something I would worry about."

"Thank you, Doctor," I said, turning around and composing myself.

"My pleasure. I'll see you in about 4 weeks for your 12-week scan. You can schedule it up front before you leave. Please call my office and let me know if you need anything between now and then. It was great meeting you, Dominic. Congratulations, you guys."

He stepped out of the room and closed the door behind him.

"I'm so sorry, I didn't mean to laugh," I said softly, reaching over to take his hands. "Are you sure you're okay?"

"I think so," he sighed, not looking at me yet.

"Let's go schedule the next ultrasound, and then we'll get something to take your mind off this for a little bit, okay?"

He nodded and took my hand as I led him down the hallway and took care of everything with the receptionist. We got to the parking lot and I wasn't sure that he was in any position to drive, so I had him get in my car and took him to Rockin' Rooster. If there was anything that could help right now, a turtle pecan brownie would do it.

It was quiet when we walked inside, aside from the rooster that crowed to greet us. I was happy that Abby was working today because I really needed to talk to someone about what happened and that we weren't expecting just one baby but two. Abby and Nate were sitting at one of the tables by the register and I could tell they both knew something was wrong the moment their faces went from happy to falling when they saw Dominic.

"What happened?" Abby asked, rushing over to hug me.

"Nothing, we're fine. I'll tell you guys in a minute, but for now, can we get two brownies?"

"Yeah, sure. Coming right up." She studied us before she rushed to the display case to grab them.

We sat at the table they were sitting at and waited for Abby to return.

"Do we need anything else? Coffee? Whiskey? The sex cake?"

"No!" Dominic yelled, a terrified look on his face after the word sex.

"Just a few glasses of water would be great, thanks," I called over to her while keeping my eyes on Dominic.

She returned a few minutes later and set the brownies in front of us before taking her seat next to Nate and waiting for us to share the news.

"Do you want to tell them, or do you want me to?" I asked Dominic quietly, turning my head to face him.

He locked eyes with me, and for a moment, it felt like it was just us in the room. He inhaled deeply, letting his shoulders rise and fall with his breath.

"I have super sperm." He shrugged and let his hands fall to the table.

Abby pulled her brows together in confusion while Nate grinned like an idiot.

"Congratulations, man," he said, not even knowing what he was actually congratulating Dominic on.

"Thanks," Dominic replied, staring down at the table. "They were so aggressive that they broke through the condom and knocked her up twice. The doctor said that I don't have to worry about it happening again right now, but I don't know. I kinda don't trust them anymore."

"I think you're just in shock right now, baby," I said softly, gently squeezing his arm. "It's going to be okay, I promise. Why don't you have some brownie while I talk to Abby and Nate?"

He nodded and lifted it to his mouth, taking a big bite.

Abby raised her eyebrows at me impatiently.

"So, um, yeah. We're having twins. Fraternal."

Both of their jaws dropped at the same time.

"Twins?" Abby asked in disbelief.

I pressed my lips into a smile and nodded.

"Fraternal means?" Nate asked, looking at Abby and then at me.

"Two separate eggs were fertilized by two separate sperm," I answered.

"Super sperm," Dominic added before taking another bite.

I shrugged because he wasn't really wrong about that.

"Fuck," Nate exhaled, leaning back in his chair.

Abby elbowed him in his side as discreetly as possible.

"What?" he complained, rubbing at the sore spot. "I didn't say it was bad; I just imagine the surprise must be a lot to process right now."

"It is," I agreed. "We obviously weren't expecting to get pregnant, to begin with, let alone have twins."

"This is so crazy," Abby gushed, her face softening into happiness. "I'm so excited for you guys! I can't believe there are going to be two new babies for me to love on!"

"Don't you mean *three?*" Nate whispered, rubbing his hand across her stomach while resting his forehead against hers.

"Three?" Dominic blurted out, choking on a bite of brownie.

"Don't worry, man, you didn't knock anyone else up. You're good," Nate assured him.

"Abby?" I asked, lifting my eyebrows as I waited for her response.

"*Someone* is as good with keeping secrets as I am," she teased. "We found out this morning."

"You're pregnant?!" I squealed excitedly, getting up to hug my sister.

She nodded and wrapped her arms around me.

"We're going to have babies together?!"

"Yeah, except you had to go and beat me by having two at the same time," she teased.

I placed my hand on her stomach and smiled.

"How far along are you?"

"I'm guessing around four to five weeks. I have an appointment later this week to get my bloodwork done, and then we'll schedule an ultrasound."

"You know, Doctor Nicoli said that it was more common to have twins with geriatric pregnancies," I said, grinning so much that my face hurt. "Maybe we can have twins together!"

"Uh uh," Nate said, standing up and pushing a hand between us to separate us. "Abby, you better move away from her."

"Why?" She laughed, swatting at him.

"Because I'm fully on board with having another baby, but I don't think I can be tag teamed. That's two on one. I'm too old for that, Abby. You better move away from her in case it's contagious or something."

She rolled her eyes, and I joined her. These men of ours were definitely going to keep us busy with their cute little freakouts.

Thirty-One
Dominic

Jane and Abby had arranged babysitters for the evening so the four of us could go to dinner and celebrate the news before we told everyone else. I was kinda relieved when Nate freaked out about twins, but then that was short-lived because I was still the only one between the two of us who was actually having them.

Jane and I had taken the day off from work, allowing us to hang out at her house for a bit before the kids got home from school. I went home to spend some time with Olivia before she left to pick them up, mainly because we didn't want to explain why I was at their house with their mom instead of at school teaching Mikey.

I knew it was going to be hard keeping this secret from my mom because she had always been able to read me like a book. Normally, I wouldn't care because I trusted that she could keep a secret; however, now the problem was that she was best friends with Jane's parents, and I didn't know whether she'd be able to keep this news to herself. The last thing I wanted was for Jane's parents to find out from my parents instead of from Jane.

My parents knew I was going to dinner with Jane, Abby, and Nate tonight, but they didn't know why. Nor did they ask, which was great because I hadn't been able to think up a lie on the short drive home from Jane's house. As soon as I pulled into the driveway, my phone vibrated. I pulled it out, hoping to find a text message from Jane but clenched my jaw when I saw Rebecca's name on the caller ID instead.

"What do you want?" I answered, gripping the steering wheel tightly. My parents had probably already heard me pull up, but they would give it a few minutes before they came outside looking for me.

"Well, that's no way to answer your phone."

"It is when you call. What do you want, Rebecca?"

"We need to talk."

"There's nothing to talk about. If you want money, I can't help you."

"I want to see my daughter," she said with the same sweetness in her voice that she used to use to manipulate me to get whatever she wanted.

"No fucking way."

"What?" she gasped. "You would really keep a mother from her child?"

"You walked away from her the day she was born. Don't you dare try to pull that bullshit with me. You left and never looked back."

"I made a mistake, and now I'm trying to fix it."

"No."

She sighed heavily into the phone, and I could hear the irritation building on the other side.

"Why are you like this?" she asked hastily.

"Like what?"

"So mean. Controlling. A bit of dick if you ask me."

"Well, I didn't," I snapped at her. "But *you* made me this way, Rebecca. You and that nasty drug habit of yours."

"I'm clean. Have been for over a year."

"Bullshit."

"You don't have to believe me, but a judge will."

"What the fuck are you talking about?" My knuckles were white from how hard I was gripping the steering wheel to control my anger.

"Judges don't like to keep their kids from their mothers, Dominic. You know that. Especially when that mother has turned her life around and is trying. I really don't want to do it this way, but if you're not going to leave me any other choice than to—"

"You come anywhere near us, and I'll have your ass thrown into jail. Do you understand me?"

I didn't wait for her to answer before I hung up the phone and tossed it onto the passenger seat beside me. I rested my head on the steering wheel and tried to push away the anger and hatred that was seeping through me from talking to her. There was no way in hell I was going to go inside and hold my daughter while those toxic feelings were still so close to the surface.

Once my blood pressure had come down some, I took a few deep breaths and went inside. Olivia was awake and sitting in her highchair while my mom watched her eat the banana slices she'd given her.

"Hey, honey. Everything okay?" she asked the moment she saw me.

Thankfully, I no longer had to lie about being stressed about the twins. Thanks to Rebecca, I had a valid reason for being in the mood I was in, which meant I could keep the pregnancy a secret for a little while longer.

"Yeah, I just got off the phone with Rebecca."

My mom's eyes nearly bulged out of her head while my dad shook his head angrily.

"What did she want?" she asked quietly, lifting another small piece of banana to Olivia's mouth.

"You don't want to know."

She arched a brow and asked the question she didn't dare to speak.

I nodded and pulled out a chair beside my daughter, already feeling calmer just being next to her.

"Hey baby girl, how's my cutie pie doing?"

She smiled at me and lifted her chubby little fingers to offer me some of the mushed banana she'd been playing with on the tray.

"No, thank you," I laughed, rubbing my fingers gently across the top of her hand. "But someone is going to need a bath tonight."

"Grandma is on top of it," my mom said, giving her another piece.

"I'm just glad to see her eating different foods. Thanks again for watching her tonight, by the way."

"No problem," my dad said, sitting beside my mom in the empty seat. "Doug said they were going to take their grandkids out for pizza tonight and asked if we wanted to join them. I've gotta say, I'm really enjoying this whole grandpa thing. It's the fun of being a parent without all the responsibility." He winked playfully, but I felt my face fall when I thought about how much work it was going to be having twins on top of Olivia still being little. Thankfully, Mikey and Sally were older and could help out some, but still, a lot would be piling up on us soon.

"You sure you're okay?" my mom asked, narrowing her eyes as she studied me. "You seem off to me."

"I'm fine," I lied. "Just tired. I'm going to go take a quick shower before dinner."

"Okay, I'm going to clean her up and then get her down for a quick nap," my mom answered as I stood up. "Oh, I forgot to ask how your conference went today. You said it was a leadership course, right?"

I swallowed hard, pushing past the ball lodged in my throat that I got every time I lied to my mom.

"Yeah. It was great. I learned a lot about what it takes to lead a team." I forced a smile and rushed out of the room before she could ask any more questions.

By the time I finished shaving and cleaned up, Olivia was already down for her nap. I decided to go ahead and go to the restaurant early when Nate texted me and asked if I wanted to meet him for a beer before the girls got there. Abby had to work until five, then Jane was going to pick her up and they would meet us at six. I think they needed some sister time to talk about things, especially since the restaurant was only fifteen minutes away from everything in Beaumont Creek, yet they needed an hour before they would be there.

But it was fine with me because I definitely needed a few minutes to clear my head before they got there. Nate was already sitting at the bar when I got there but hadn't ordered yet.

"Hey, thanks for the invite," I said, clapping a hand on his shoulder before I took the barstool beside him.

"Not a problem. Thanks for meeting me for a drink. I wasn't sure if you wanted beer or something harder before the girls got here."

"I'll stick with beer. After this morning, I don't need to give Jane any more reasons to be embarrassed by me."

"I doubt she's embarrassed," Nate said as he lifted his hand to wave down the bartender. "Trust me, we've all done crazy things when we get big news like that. I had the nerve to ask Abby whether the baby was mine when she told me she was pregnant."

"Yikes, how did that go?"

"Well, she slapped me, which I deserved. But in all fairness, she had started dating some guy her mom was trying to set her up with, so I didn't know if they had done anything. I should have found a better way to ask, but it is what it is. She forgave me and confirmed she never even slept with the guy."

The bartender made his way down and took our order.

Once we had our beers, we found a table in the corner away

from the noise of the TVs hanging above the bar and sat down.

"So, how are you doing?" he asked, leaning back in his seat.

"I don't know, man. I thought I was fine, but then, out of nowhere, I wasn't."

"It's a lot to take in."

"That's for damn sure," I laughed. "You know, I was excited when Jane told me she was pregnant. I even did well at the ultrasound when he stuck the thing in, you know."

He nodded.

"Yeah, I freaked out when I saw the doctor do it to Abby. I don't think there's anything that can brace you for that."

"Right? No matter how prepared I tried to be, I still wasn't. Twins weren't even on my radar, so I felt like I was letting Jane down left and right. How is she going to feel having a baby with someone who passes out in the doctor's office and freaks out about twins?"

"Honestly, I think most guys would have had a similar reaction, don't be so hard on yourself."

I sighed and lifted my beer to my lips, allowing the cold liquid to take the edge off for a moment.

"I don't want to disappoint her," I admitted. "I want to be there for her and help her with the babies. With Mikey and Sally. I want us to be a family and figure this out together as we go, but I worry that she's going to feel like she's getting four new kids—the twins, Olivia, and me."

Nate took a drink and studied me for a moment before

lowering his glass and cocking his head to the side.

"Are you planning to walk out on her and leave her to do this by herself?"

"No," I answered immediately.

"Are you going to leave all the big decisions up to her and not pull your weight with the kids?"

"No."

"Are you planning to make her do all of the disciplining while you get to be the fun parent?"

"Hell no."

He lifted his beer and waited for me to raise mine to his.

"Then you're already steps ahead of her ex-husband," he said, clanking our glasses together. "You've got this."

Thirty-Two

Jane

"I'm so nervous, my ass is sweating," I hissed quietly at Dominic as he stood next to me at the stove, helping with dinner. Tonight was the night we were finally going to tell the kids that we were dating, and I was a complete mess. Abby tried to comfort me and assure me that it was likely just the pregnancy hormones that were messing with my head, but I knew it was because everything was about to get even more real.

Two weeks had passed since we found out about the twins, and I was already at the ten-week mark. We agreed that we would ease the kids into the news about us dating tonight, and then we would tell them about the babies in a few weeks. We'd gone back and forth about whether to tell them everything tonight, but I wasn't sure if it would be too much for them.

Mikey had been doing better lately after we sat down and had a talk about his dad and I was worried that this would set him back again. While this had nothing to do with Rick or his fiancé, it was a significant change for me, and I didn't want him to think that I no longer had time for him or that he might be overlooked when the babies came.

"It's going to be fine," he assured me, gently rubbing my back before the kids came in for dinner. "And your ass looks fine too. Though I can check it later if you want me to."

I grinned at the invite and felt my cheeks burn.

"While I would love that, maybe you should go check on Olivia. She's been alone with Mikey and Sally for twenty minutes, and no one is crying. I'm starting to worry about how quiet it is."

"Alright. But we do have to get used to them being together without worrying so much. It'll take some time, but we'll get there."

"I know," I sighed heavily, stirring the pot of noodles for the mac and cheese I was making.

Since it was Friday night, Dominic had suggested that we pick up food somewhere, but I insisted on cooking the kids' favorite foods instead. Was I trying to butter them up? Absolutely.

The macaroni and cheese was for Olivia, though I wasn't sure she needed any bribing. She was good as long as she had toys and her sippy cup of milk. I made sliders and tater tots for Mikey, and for Sally, I prepared her favorite dish—chicken parmigiana with angel hair pasta. Was it too much food and a lot of work? Hell yes. But they were worth it, and I wanted that to be the message loud and clear tonight—no matter what changed in our lives, they would still be just as important to me as they always have been.

I opened the oven to check on the food and then went back to stirring the pots on the stove. Dominic laughed when I asked him if there was something special he wanted to eat and then said he'd eat whatever I gave him. Then he offered a dirty suggestion of what he *really wanted to eat,* and I reminded him that was how I got pregnant in the first place.

"Dinner will be ready in ten minutes," I yelled, making sure everyone could hear me. "Go wash your hands and get in here."

I took the dishes out of the oven, set them on the table, and then finished preparing the rest of the food. By the time the kids came in and sat down, everything was ready.

"Wow, Mom, that's a lot of food." Mikey smiled and sat down, immediately reaching for a slider.

"I wanted to make a special dinner for us tonight," I said, tousling his hair before I sat down at the other end of the table opposite Dominic.

I grabbed the pan with the chicken parm and put some on Sally's plate before adding the noodles. Dominic took care of getting Olivia's food, and it felt like this was some sort of norm for us, sitting down and eating dinner as a family.

Once everyone had their food, I looked down at my plate, trying to gather the courage to do this. It was harder than telling my parents that I had a boyfriend in high school, which suddenly made me laugh.

Everyone turned to look at me, Dominic's eyebrow raised slightly with a deliciously sexy lopsided grin.

"Sorry," I said nervously, folding my hands in my lap under the table to keep from fidgeting. "I was just thinking about something that happened at work, and it made me laugh."

I knew that Dominic immediately picked up on my lie, but the kids didn't give it a second thought as they started eating. I looked across the table at him and shrugged. He discreetly pointed at himself, silently asking if I wanted him to do it instead.

I shook my head and took a deep, steadying breath in. I needed to be the one to do it, not him.

Releasing the breath slowly, I counted to five and then began.

"The reason that we're having a special dinner tonight is because there's something that mommy wants to tell you guys," I said, surprised at how calmly I could get the words out.

"Are you pregnant?" Sally asked, immediately turning to look at me with a smile.

I opened my mouth to say no, then quickly shut it because I couldn't bring myself to lie to her.

"Ummm."

The words wouldn't come out, no matter how hard I tried.

She frowned, just as confused by my lack of a response as Mikey was. He turned to face me as well, and I wished the earth would open up and swallow me.

I looked up, panicked, and found Dominic smiling gently at me with his elbows resting on the table and his hands steepled. He nodded, giving me the strength I needed to go on.

"Well," I paused. "Yes. I am pregnant."

"Is it dad's baby?" Mikey asked.

"What? No. Of course not," I said with a little too much aggression before I realized that it was a perfectly logical guess for him, given that they didn't know that Dominic and I had been seeing each other. "I'm sorry, honey. I didn't mean to react that way. But no, it's not your father's baby."

"So, whose is it?" Sally asked, setting her fork down to focus on the conversation.

Mikey turned to look at Dominic and then Olivia, and I

could tell that he had figured it out.

"But you guys aren't even dating," Mikey said, leaving Sally completely in the dark.

"Well, that's what I wanted to talk to you guys about," I replied, trying to take control of the conversation again. "Dominic and I have been dating, but we didn't want to say anything until we were sure that this was something serious."

"But you guys are already having a baby," Mikey objected. Sometimes I hated how freaking smart he was for his age. "Isn't that serious?"

"Yes," I replied easily.

"So, have you guys been dating the entire time he's been coming over for dinner?" Mikey's tone changed, but I didn't recognize any anger in it, so I answered his questions as honestly as possible.

"Yes and no," I admitted. "We've been interested in each other for a few months and have had a few dates. But that's not the only reason that I've invited them over for dinner or to hang out. I enjoy his friendship, and you guys seemed to as well."

Mikey nodded and then looked at Dominic.

"We weren't trying to hide anything from you guys," Dominic said, acknowledging both Mikey and Sally as he looked at them. "We wanted to be sure that we knew what this thing was between us before we told anyone else."

"But my mom's pregnant," Mikey said.

"She is." Dominic smiled at me and then addressed Mikey again. "It wasn't something that we planned to happen, but we're both very excited about it. We hope that you guys will be too."

"I'm going to be a big sister?" Sally asked with a grin that showed off the tooth she'd recently lost.

"You are," I said, reaching over and gently squeezing her hand. "And you're going to be a big brother again."

"What about Olivia? Does this make her our sister?" Mikey asked, looking at the sweet girl with cheese all over her face.

Dominic and I looked at each other, unsure of what to say. Perhaps we should have discussed this before having this conversation with the kids. They had more questions than I was prepared to answer. Not only that, I didn't have the answer to some of them.

"Olivia will be a big sister to the new baby," Dominic answered carefully. "And she loves spending time with you guys. Right now, she's too little to understand what any of this means. But what do you want? Do you want her to be your sister?"

Without thinking twice about it, both Mikey and Sally answered *yes* simultaneously.

My cheeks split as I grinned, already feeling relieved about how they were handling all of this. There was still the last bit of news we needed to share with them and now seemed as good of a time as any.

"I'm really happy that you guys are okay with this. It means a lot to both me and Dominic because we love each other very much. And as our family grows, it's incredibly important to us that you guys—all three of you—know how much you are loved. Just because we're adding to our family, it doesn't mean that we love you guys any less or that you're not going to get as much attention from us. Okay?"

They both nodded and then went to start eating again.

"There is one more thing that we need to tell you guys," I said quickly, letting the words rush out of my mouth before I could rethink them.

"Are you guys getting married too?" Sally asked.

My eyes widened as I looked up at Dominic, hoping her comment didn't freak him out.

"Not yet," he laughed. "But maybe someday, if that's okay with you guys."

"Yeah, that would be okay," Mikey said, giving me a wink.

"The other thing is that it's not just *one* baby. We're having twins, which means that mommy is carrying two babies in her tummy."

"*Two*?!" Sally shrieked.

I nodded and watched the smile spread across her face.

"I'm gonna be busy," Mikey said before lifting his slider to his mouth and taking a bite.

"Why's that?" I asked.

"Because soon I'll have two more people to look after and protect. Before it was just you and Sally; now there's Olivia—since I get to be her big brother. That's already three people, and then add in two more babies. I'm going to have a lot of butt-kicking to do on the playground." He grinned as he chewed his bite, looking mighty proud of himself.

"Don't worry, I've got your back," Dominic said, meeting Mikey's fist for a new fist bump/handshake thing they'd started.

The weight on my shoulders was now lighter, and I felt better about the kids knowing everything. They handled things better than I had thought they would, though maybe I hadn't given them enough credit, to begin with.

We ate dinner, talked, and laughed before going to the living room for a family game night because that's what we were now, a family.

Thirty-Three
Dominic

"We're going to a barbeque at Doug and Rhonda's for Father's Day. You should come with us," my mom said as she shuffled about the house, picking up Olivia's toys while she napped. Even though I was off for the summer, they still insisted on watching her for me and keeping the same routine we had during the school year.

It was weird getting used to sudden freedom, but I found myself spending that time looking for a new house that Jane and I could move into together before the babies got here. We hadn't talked about it yet since I didn't want to overwhelm her right now. The kids had taken the news well and, over the past few weeks, had gotten used to us all spending more time together.

We took turns hanging out at her house as well as mine, but I knew that it was still a lot for her to handle since it was so different from her norm. Plus, the kids were officially on summer break and we had our next ultrasound coming up, so there was a lot on her plate as it was.

"I don't know, I'll see." I hadn't talked to Jane about what their plans were for Father's Day and if she was taking the kids to Rick's. I assumed she would, but then again, he had been even more distant with them, so I wasn't so sure.

"I don't want you spending the day by yourself. Doug just

caught a bunch of catfish, and they're going to fry them. I know how much you love fried catfish," she continued with a sing-song tone.

I picked up the last few toys and put them in the bins, then joined her on the couch. My phone started ringing, so I pulled it out of my pocket and sighed heavily. I pressed the button to ignore the call and sat it on the couch beside me.

"Everything alright?" she asked, glancing at my phone and then up at me.

"Yeah, just a telemarketer."

"I hate those calls. Half the time you can't even hear anything, and the rest of the time it's a damn robot. I'm pretty sure they do it so they can track where people are and whether they're home to answer their phones. Then they send their goons to break into your house and steal everything."

"I don't think that's how any of it works, Mom," I laughed, not bothering to tell her that it was Rebecca.

It had been a few weeks since the last time she called and I ignored it. It was irritating that she wouldn't get the message after I told her two months ago to stop calling me. But one thing about her, she didn't stop until she got what she wanted.

Whether or not she really wanted to see Olivia and try to be in her life again was impossible to know. I didn't trust Rebecca as far as I could throw her, and I knew that everything with her revolved around drugs. Even if she was clean again, like she claimed to, it would only be a matter of time before she relapsed again. I hated to be so pessimistic, but she had already shown me her true colors so many times before so I knew what to expect from her.

We watched TV for a bit, or more so my mom devoured every ounce of drama on the soap opera while I browsed more houses on Zillow. There were a few that I really liked and had bookmarked, but I wasn't sure that they would still be available by the time I sat down and talked to Jane about them.

While I scrolled through pictures of a newly renovated house close to the school, a new text message popped up from Jane.

Jane: Do you have plans on Sunday?

Me: Father's Day? Nope. But my mom did just invite me to a BBQ at your parent's house.

Jane: That's so funny because I was going to see if you wanted to go with us.

Me: Are the kids not going to Rick's?

Jane: (angry emoji)

Jane: No, he's going to be out of town looking at wedding venues with his fiancé.

Me: On Father's Day?

Jane: (Hands up, shrugging emoji)

Me: What an ass.

Jane: You're telling me.

Jane: You don't have to go to my parent's house. I was going to see if you wanted to do something else instead. I can cook, or we can take you out. Your pick.

Me: Do you want to go to your parent's house?

Jane: Yes and no. I haven't told them that I'm pregnant

yet and don't know how much longer I'll be able to hide it. I'm starting to get a bump.

Me: I love your bump. It's fucking sexy.

Jane: Thanks, baby. But I know my mom is going to be mad that I haven't told her before now, so that's why I don't want to go. I want to see my dad, though. We have gifts the kids made for him.

Me: How sweet and thoughtful.

Jane: They made some for you, too (winking emoji)

Me: (crying emoji) They like me. They really, really like me!

Jane: Of course they do. Who wouldn't?

Me: Your mom when she finds out that I knocked you up with twins.

Jane: I think Abby is going to tell them that she's pregnant that day too.

Me: Is it a race to see who does it first? Because I could get on board with that. I'm quite competitive.

Jane: I know, that's what I'm worried about lol. You and Nate trying to beat each other in who can announce it first.

Me: Well, we're still beating them. Two to one.

Jane: You're a dork. But think about it and let me know what you want to do. Maybe we can do the BBQ for lunch, and then I can make you a special dinner at my house?

Me: Is it your pussy? Because I would love to eat that.

Jane: You just had it last night. And this morning.

Me: What can I say? It's my favorite meal.

Jane: (blushing emoji)

Me: I'm good doing whatever you want to do.

Jane: I can take that so many ways… (wink emoji)

Me: And I'll satisfy every single one. But really, I'm good going to your parent's for lunch and then eating you out for dinner.

Jane: The kids will be there, so you'll have to wait for dessert.

Me: Fine. It's worth the wait.

Jane: Are you going to tell your parents before Sunday?

Me: I don't know. Should I?

Jane: They're best friends with my parents, so maybe we just tell them together? That way, no one has hurt feelings that someone knew before them.

Me: Sounds like a plan.

Jane: Alright, I have to get back to work. I'll see you when I get home.

Me: I'll be there. Have a great day, baby.

Jane: You too. Love you!

Me: Love you three times (three heart emojis)

****

When I picked Jane up Sunday morning, I nearly choked on my coffee when I saw the flowy sundress she was wearing. The soft pink fabric hinted at the curves I knew she had but was loose enough to help hide her baby bump. But even still, I couldn't help but wish for a few minutes alone with her and a strong breeze to blow it up so I could see underneath it.

It turned out that it wasn't just pregnant Jane who was horny these days—I also couldn't get my fill of her. Every time her body changed even a little bit, I was obsessed with it. I wanted to devour her 24/7 but kept my restraint since we had three kids who didn't need to see that.

"Good morning," I said, smiling at her and the kids as they came out of the house and piled into my truck. I'd kept it running with the windows down so I could keep an eye on Olivia as Mikey and Sally got situated next to her.

I pulled Jane in for a hug and a quick kiss before opening the door for her.

"You look incredible," I whispered, feeling her giggle against me.

"Thank you."

"It makes it really hard not to run you back into the house and strip this thin fabric off you."

"Well, if you did that, we would have to explain to the kids and my parents why we're late."

"Ugh," I groaned, pouting my bottom lip out. "You're no fun."

"You can have fun later," she laughed, taking my hand as I helped her into the truck.

The drive to her parent's house was quick and not long enough for me to prepare myself for telling everyone our news today, even though I'd known that we were going to do it for a few days.

My parents were already there by the time we got there, but Abby and Nate were running late, according to Jane's mother.

"Go ahead and head outside; your father is manning the grill," Rhonda said, kissing Jane's cheek before hugging me and kissing mine.

The kids were already outside, wishing their grandpa a happy father's day as we followed behind them. My father reached for Olivia, his eyes lighting up the way they always did when he got to hold his grandbaby. Not that he didn't see her often—my mom just had a hard time sharing her.

"Happy Father's Day," I said, pulling him in for a hug as we tried not to squish my daughter.

"Happy Father's Day to you too, son."

I walked around and said hello, then joined Jane at a table in the shade while the kids drew pictures on the concrete patio with chalk.

"Are you sure you want to do this today?" Jane asked through gritted teeth so no one could read her lips.

"Yup. You?"

She looked at me and shook her head before laughing.

"No, but we have to."

"It'll be fine, I promise."

"What will be fine?" my mom asked, startling us as she squeezed into the seat on the other side of me.

"Nothing," I lied, giving my mom the look to stop asking questions.

Thankfully, Nate and Abby chose that moment to show up, and the attention got shifted to them as they came outside with Penny wearing a jacket. Rhonda immediately went over and picked her up after Nate set her down, scowling at the outfit choice.

"Why is she wearing a coat when it's already so warm? She's going to roast."

"Take it off then," Abby said, watching as Nate stood beside her with his arm wrapped around her waist.

Rhonda picked Penny up and started fussing with the buttons and zippers.

"Maybe have Dad help you," Abby suggested, not bothering to assist her mother.

Doug walked over and unzipped the jacket while Rhonda held Penny against her chest with her back to her. As soon as it was open, he stopped and stared at the shirt she was wearing. He covered his mouth with his hand and then looked over at Abby with tears in his eyes.

"Really?" he asked.

Abby nodded, and moisture licked at the corner of her eyes as well.

"What? What's going on?" Rhonda demanded, turning Penny to face her so she could see what had gotten Doug so choked up. As she moved her, we caught a glimpse of the t-shirt with the words *Big Sister* printed on it.

Her eyes quickly scanned Penny's shirt before she looked up, a shocked expression on her face.

"Baby! Baby!" Penny said, squirming until Rhonda put her down.

Doug reached down and finished taking her coat off so she could run over to where Sally and Mikey were still coloring with chalk. Olivia had joined them, and it was fun seeing all the kids together.

"You guys are expecting again?" Rhonda said excitedly.

"We are," Abby replied as Nate kissed her forehead. "Penny is going to be a big sister."

Everyone took turns congratulating them before they sat down to eat. I wasn't sure when Jane wanted to share our news or whether she had reconsidered altogether.

Our mothers were both busy, bustling around to get the food out before they would sit down. The kids waited impatiently for the all-clear to start eating.

"Are you sure you don't need help, Mom?" Jane asked, getting ready to get up when her mom placed her hand on her shoulder to stop her.

"No, dear, I'm fine."

She rushed back into the kitchen and then returned a few minutes later with bottles of champagne.

"Alright, the food is ready. Who wants a mimosa?" Rhonda asked, peeling the wrapper off the bottle before popping it open.

"I'll have one," my mom answered, taking the glass she was handed. There were bottles of assorted juice spread out along the table and charcuterie boards filled with meats, cheeses, and fruits.

"We know that Abby won't be having one, but don't worry—I made sure there was plenty of bacon after learning the news."

"Thank you, Mom," Abby said. "But this time, I can't stand bacon. It seems this baby wants egg rolls." She shrugged and leaned into Nate, who couldn't seem to keep his hands off of her.

"My mom has been eating a lot of jerky and peanut M&M's," Sally said, not realizing what she had said. "I guess each baby wants something different."

Jane's face went white as a sheet as she stared at Sally while Rhonda stared at Jane.

"What?" Rhonda asked.

Jane rubbed her lips together and then looked helplessly at me. She'd already been the one to tell the kids, so I didn't mind telling our parents. I pulled her close to me and wrapped my arms around her shoulder while everyone stared at us.

"Well, this Father's Day, I have more to celebrate," I said, smiling at Olivia as my dad held her. "I've been blessed to be a dad again, this time to two babies. Jane and I are expecting twins."

My mother gasped loudly and almost spat her mimosa across the table before she was able to cover her mouth with her napkin. My father's face lit up as he grinned proudly at us. And Jane's parents—well, Jane's parents seemed to be in disbelief. I couldn't necessarily blame them, given we had just shared the news that we were dating a few weeks ago after telling Mikey and Sally.

Doug was the first to respond with congratulations and a handshake from across the table, while Rhonda continued standing and took a swig right from the bottle of champagne.

"Isn't this great, honey?" Doug asked, standing beside her and pulling the bottle away. "We're going to be grandparents again!"

"*Three* new babies?" she asked, looking from Jane to Abby, both of them nodding. "But you guys just started dating. And you're pregnant already? When is this all happening? When are you girls due?" Rhonda asked as she let Doug pull her seat out for her and sat down.

"My due date is December 31st, but the doctor thinks there's a chance they could come sooner. It's common for twins to come before their due date," Jane explained.

Rhonda's eyes narrowed as she did the math in her head.

"How long have you known you were pregnant?" she asked. "Because it was only a few weeks ago that we found out you guys were dating. And now babies are coming. Where are you all going to live?"

Jane's cheeks flushed as she tucked a strand of hair behind her ear.

"I've known since I was about 4 weeks along." Jane chose to answer one question and ignore the others.

"How far are you now?" her dad asked.

"Twelve."

"You've known for *two months* and kept this from us? Why didn't you mention it when you told us about the two of you?" Rhonda asked, the disappointment in her voice evident. She looked at my parents and then at me. "Did you guys know?"

"No, Dominic didn't say anything until now," my mom answered, though there was nothing but happiness in her voice. "But we also know that he'll tell us stuff when he's ready. Just like when he finally confessed that they were seeing each other. We'd guessed all along that they were, but it was nice when he finally admitted it."

"I didn't—*we*—didn't say anything," Jane said sternly, "because we wanted to get through the first trimester. There's more of a risk with being older and carrying twins. We didn't want to tell anyone until we felt more comfortable after the twelve-week ultrasound."

"And everything is fine?" Doug asked, holding Penny in his lap.

"Yes, everything looks great," Jane answered with a smile. "We're all doing well and very excited about this."

"Okay," Rhonda sighed, reaching for her glass that had been filled with champagne. "And when are you due, Abby?"

"I'm due January 21st."

"Wow, you guys are almost due at the same time!" my mom said, lifting her glass to take a drink. "How exciting!"

Our moms started talking about baby showers and all of the things they wanted to get for the babies they'd just found out about a few minutes ago while everyone else started eating. I leaned in close and kissed Jane's cheek.

"I told you it would be okay," I said softly, feeling her hand rest on my thigh.

"I know. Now I'm just counting down the hours until I can take you home and give you your Father's Day gift." She wiggled her eyebrows suggestively, making my body ache with what I hoped she meant by that.

Thirty-Four

Jane

Father's Day went off better than I had expected. Maybe it was easier because I didn't have to fight with Rick about him taking the kids, but I still couldn't help the hurt that radiated through me that they didn't get to spend any time with him or give him the gifts they'd made.

I also couldn't shake the feeling that they were already more attached to Dominic than they were to their own father. It was weird, but then again, he spent more time with them and actually took an interest in the things they liked. He'd recently bought a new football for Mikey after he found out that he'd lost his the last time he went to his dad's house. I knew that it wasn't lost, but that Rick had hidden it or gotten rid of it, so he didn't have to play with him.

Dominic also found an antique dollhouse at one of the thrift shops and asked if he could get it and fix it up for Sally. My heart swelled at his generosity, but it nearly exploded when I saw how much time he'd spent fixing it up. Not only was the house cleaned up with a fresh coat of paint, but there were also little things he'd added that were totally Sally. Like the furniture he'd "found" that included dog beds for Barbie's pets—which just happened to be her favorite.

We were spending nearly all of our time together and everyone seemed to be happy. The only thing that was still hard was that we were splitting our time between my house and his when it would be easier if we had one place for all of us. My house was bigger than his, but there wasn't enough room for all of us. While there was a guest bedroom for Olivia, there wouldn't be any room for the twins when they got here.

Not only would one house make it easier, so we didn't have to shuffle the kids back and forth, but it would also be great not to sneak around after I dropped the kids off at my parent's house for quickies with Dominic before work. Last night, we'd waited until the kids were asleep—including Olivia, who now had a permanent Pack 'N Play that stayed at my house, and then I gave him the best blow job of his life. His words, not mine. Though I did put a lot more effort into it than I had ever before.

On my way to work this morning, I stopped by Rockin' Rooster and grabbed a vanilla latte, determined that today was going to be a wonderful day. Our families knew that we were together and having a baby, so I didn't have to keep anything a secret anymore.

I was in such a good mood that I'd even stopped by the bakery and grabbed a dozen glazed donuts for the office. I set them down at the nurse's desk and grinned when I saw everyone rush over.

"You're a lifesaver, thank you, Doctor Hughes," Sabrina said as she snatched one before grabbing a chart and sitting down behind the desk. "My blow dryer died this morning, and then everything else that could go wrong did, so I didn't have time to eat breakfast."

"Maybe you should just get rid of the blow dryer," Nick said, coming up behind her and grabbing another chart.

"The curly hair looks great on you."

"Thank you." She tucked her chin to keep him from seeing her blush.

When he walked off to go to the patient's room, I leaned in and whispered to her so no one could hear. I didn't want to add to her day by embarrassing her.

"I think Nick likes you," I said, loving how her cheeks darkened.

"Really?" She scrunched her nose like she didn't believe me.

"Absolutely. I've noticed him watching you lately and then the comment about your hair. He's totally into you." I tapped my fingers on the desk and then stopped talking when he came out of the room a few minutes later. "Also— your hair really does look great. I love the curls!"

I grabbed the chart he handed me and headed into the room, leaving them to have a few minutes alone at the desk. Love was in the air and I was more than happy to help someone else find the same joy that I'd found with Dominic.

The rest of the day was slow and uneventful, probably because I couldn't wait to go home and see Dominic. Once we were done for the day, I stopped by Surf 'N Shack to pick up dinner since I was too tired to cook. It seemed that being pregnant with twins really was sucking out any energy that I had before and I hated that I was starting to rely so much on eating out these days. Thankfully, Dominic volunteered to cook fairly often. He was an exceptional chef that could even get MY picky eaters to clear their plates. But I wanted to give us a break tonight because the sooner we were done with dinner, the sooner I could cuddle in his arms while the kids played.

I stood in line, waiting to place my order when I noticed the slump in Capshaw's shoulders and the frown on his face. The woman in front of me paid for her meal and then moved to the side to wait for her drink. I moved forward, waiting patiently for him to acknowledge me.

"Hey, Jane. What can I get you?"

My face fell from the sad tone in his voice.

"Are you okay?" I asked, stepping closer and examining the dark bags under his eyes.

"Yeah, I'm fine."

"You don't look fine. You look like someone just ran over your puppy."

"Gail broke up with me."

"Oh, Capshaw. I'm so sorry. Are you okay?"

"Yeah, I will be. I just really liked this one and got my hopes up that it might turn into something more."

"I know how that is. It sucks and I hate that you have to go through it."

"Me too," he sighed. "What can I get you?"

I placed my order and then moved to the side while the kid behind the counter prepared the to-go drinks and set them in a cardboard tray.

A beautiful woman walked up behind me and I had to bite my cheek to keep from laughing at how Capshaw's eyes lit up at the woman in front of him. Maybe he'd be over this break up quicker than he thought.

I turned my head, looking around the restaurant while I waited.

"Hello," he greeted, his voice unusually deep. "What can I get for you today?"

"Hi, can I get a Diet Coke?"

"You got it. Anything else?"

"Actually, I'm new to town and trying to find someone. Maybe you can help?"

"Is he tall, dark, and handsome? Because if so, I think you just found him."

I covered my mouth with my hand and tried to hide the laughter. I thought I was the only one he used cheesy pick-up lines on.

"No," she said cautiously. "I'm looking for Dominic Rosario. He moved here a few months ago and I was hoping that you could point me in the right direction."

"Oh," Capshaw said, disappointedly. "I haven't seen him today but I can let him know you're looking for him if I see him. What's your name?"

"I'm Rebecca. His ex-wife."

My head whipped to the side so fast that I worried I might get whiplash. I stared at the beautiful woman with dark brown eyes and flawless skin as she tossed her hair over her shoulder and looked at me.

"Alright, I'll let him know if I see him. Is there anything else I can help you with?" Capshaw asked, pulling her attention back to him.

"No, that's it. Please tell him that it's urgent and that I've been trying to find him."

"Will do."

I wanted to stick around and ask Capshaw if that really happened or if I was just hallucinating that it did, but I couldn't get my brain to work. The kid behind the counter called my name and then handed me my order. My fingers trembled as I took it and stumbled to the car, wondering what in the world had just happened.

Thirty-Five
Dominic

I was walking through a house with a realtor, hoping to surprise Jane with it tonight. While I'd wanted to wait and look at houses together, this one had gone on the market today and according to the realtor, already had seven offers on it—three of them cash. I wasn't sure what we could afford or what our budget was, but I knew that this was our house. I could feel it in my bones.

My phone rang in my pocket, so I pulled it out and grinned when I saw Jane's name on the screen.

"Hey baby," I answered. "If you're calling for phone sex, now isn't really a good time." I kept my voice low while I walked into the master bedroom to keep the realtor from overhearing me.

"Your ex-wife is in town and looking for you."

My body froze as a chill ran through me.

"What?"

"I said, your ex-wife is here in Beaumont Creek. She was asking around for you at Surf 'N Shack."

"Fuck," I muttered, my blood pressure shooting through the roof. "I should have figured."

"Should have figured what?"

"That she would find me like she said she would. I knew better than to doubt her."

"What are you talking about?" Jane asked, her tone turning icy.

I shoved a hand through my hair and blew out a frustrated breath.

"She's been texting me, asking about seeing Olivia."

"And you're just now telling me about it?"

"I didn't think it was important enough to," I argued, realizing now that she was right—I should have told her.

"Your ex-wife has been reaching out to you about seeing her daughter and then shows up in town and you didn't think that was important to tell your new girlfriend who is pregnant with your babies?"

"I'm sorry, Jane—I wasn't thinking."

"No, you were. Just not about me."

"That's not fair."

"No, what's not fair is that we're supposed to be in this together, Dominic, yet you kept something like this from me."

"It was an accident, Jane. It's not like I purposely kept information from you to hurt you."

"Maybe not but that's not the point. If we're going to do this and be together, then we have to be honest with each other about everything. You don't get to choose the stuff you tell me and the stuff you keep from me—especially something like this."

"I'm sorry."

"Sorry for not telling me or sorry because I found out about it the way I did?"

"Both."

"Well I'm sorry but I think we should take some space from each other tonight. I need time to think about this."

"Please don't do that, Jane."

"Do what?"

"Put up a wall at the first sign of conflict between us. We're grownups, we should act like it and talk about this. I know that you're upset and I understand it, but it does us no good if you won't talk to me and just shut me out."

"Yeah, well, I agree. We should talk things out—before they happen. I'll talk to you tomorrow."

She hung up before I could say anything more but that didn't stop my mind from racing. I knew better than to dismiss Rebecca's threats about finding me so we could talk but I couldn't help but wonder what it was that she wanted this time.

Was she here to try to see Olivia? Was she stupid enough to take her if I didn't let her see her? Did she go through with getting a court order to get visitation rights?

"I'm sorry, I gotta go," I said to the realtor as I ran out of the house and jumped into my truck. I needed to get to my parent's house before Rebecca found them first. If she was already asking around town about me, it wouldn't take long for someone to point her in the right direction.

Thirty-Six

Jane

By the time I got home, I was exhausted. Rick had called me a few times, but I let it go to voicemail because I didn't have the energy to deal with him right now. After talking to Dominic about Rebecca, I couldn't stop thinking about what this meant for us. I knew Dominic had left her because she was a drug addict and wouldn't stay clean. She also abandoned Olivia right after she was born so she could go get high. But that didn't mean that seeing her wouldn't somehow change how he felt about her and I worried that he might want to give her another chance. She was his first love and that meant something.

The kids and I finished dinner and I felt bad for telling Dominic not to come over, but I couldn't be in the same room as him right now with everything running through my head and didn't want the kids to know something was wrong. I needed time to think about what this meant and try to get past the fact that he didn't tell me about her reaching out to him to begin with.

Maybe it wasn't my place to expect that of him, but at the same time, I'd let my guard down to make this work with him and expected that he would do the same. He knew about my struggles with Rick and I never kept him in the shadows about the things that were happening, so I expected the same courtesy from him.

My mom called later that evening, asking if they could pick up the kids for a sleepover. She knew that I had an early day tomorrow and wanted to make it easier for me with not having to get them ready and drop them off before work. I think part of it was that she could tell something was wrong when I stopped by to pick them up earlier. She didn't press and I didn't give her any details as to what was going on, which was helpful since I still felt like I had no clue.

As soon as I got off the phone with her, I got another call from Rick. Deciding that I couldn't ignore it all night, I swiped my finger across the screen and accepted it.

"Hello."

"Hey, I've been trying to reach you all afternoon," he said, irritated.

"Yeah, well, I've been busy. What's up?"

"I wanted to talk to you about something, and I need you to *not* go all *Jane* on me about it."

I rolled my eyes, hating the way he liked to use my name as a way to describe my attitude.

"No guarantees."

"I figured," he replied snarkily. "As you know, Charlie and I are getting married next month in Atlanta."

"Yes, I'm aware of it."

"And we've asked the kids to be in the wedding."

"Okay," I said slowly. This was the first I was hearing of it but I tried not to make a big deal about the last-minute notice, given I would be the one who would have to figure out their travel and take time off to make sure they got there safely.

"Well, we've also decided that we're moving there as well."

"To Atlanta."

"Yes."

"Wow. Okay. And how exactly do you expect that to work with you seeing the kids?" I planted my hand on my hip while my fingers wrapped tightly around the phone.

"I thought maybe we could amend our situation and see about having them come down for the summer."

"The summer. You want to see your kids once a year, during the summer."

It wasn't a question, just me stating the absolutely fucking ridiculous facts he'd just laid on me.

"Come on, Jane, I'm doing my best here."

"Your best? Your best? Are you kidding me right now? I know you might *think* that this is your best, but it's beyond shitty, Rick."

"You have no idea how hard this is for me, Jane. Charlie wants to be close to her parents so when the baby comes, they can help—"

"She's pregnant?"

"Yeah, I thought the kids would have told you. She's around eight weeks."

"No, they didn't mention it. Maybe you should have.

But that would mean that you would have to act like a grown-up and communicate with the other person that you originally decided to have kids with!" I was screaming, but I didn't care. "And seriously with just the summer? That's bullshit, and you know it."

"They could spend the entire summer here with us, Jane. It's not that bad. There are plenty of things for them to do and see."

"So I get to have them during the rest of the year and deal with school and homework and making sure they're happy and healthy, but you get them for the summer when there's no other responsibility? I don't fucking think so. No. The answer is no, Rick. You cannot have them for the summer. If you decide to pick your new wife and baby over your current kids, then that's on you."

"I knew you'd react this way," he sighed heavily as if *I* was the disappointment in this scenario.

"How else did you expect me to react? Did you expect me to bend over backward and give you everything you wanted? I'm sorry but I stopped doing that once we got divorced."

"No, but it would be nice if you would meet me halfway. I'm doing the best I can."

"Yeah, you've said that. I'm worried that your definition of the *best* might need some fine-tuning. You're only doing what's *best* for you, Rick. Not your kids. Not me. Just you. It's always about you and what you want. You never stop to think about anyone else."

"Well, I'll never be good enough for you, Jane. You've made that abundantly clear. Just let me know whether the kids will be here for the wedding or not. I need to give a final headcount to the caterer soon."

"I'll ask them tomorrow and let you know. "

"Fine."

He didn't bother to say goodbye before he hung up, but I didn't expect him to. It was Rick, after all.

I set my phone down and paced the kitchen, trying to wear off some of the anger that was pulsing through me. I hated how selfish he was, not that it was any surprise. He'd been that way as long as I'd known him, though I wished I would have seen it before we got married and had kids.

I knew that this was going to be hard for the kids having him move to Atlanta. They hadn't told me about the baby so it made me worried about why they'd kept it from me. I didn't want to ruin their night tonight so I would talk to them about it tomorrow.

Since I had the night to myself, I went to the bathroom and drew a warm bath, disappointed that I couldn't get it as hot as I wanted. But a warm bath was better than no bath at all. I added some Epsom salts and my favorite orange-scented bubble bath and climbed in.

I tried to relax the best I could, but I couldn't get my mind off of Rick and what an asshole he was being to the kids. They wanted their dad in their lives, yet he kept pulling away every chance he got. Then I thought about Dominic and how Rebecca had come all this way to make an effort to be in Olivia's life.

Even if they didn't want to be together again, I couldn't stop the nagging worry in the back of my mind that *I* was the thing standing between them being a family. If I weren't in the picture, maybe they could figure out a way to make it work, and Olivia wouldn't have to feel the pain that mine did from a dad who didn't want to be there. I knew Dominic loved Olivia more than anything in the world and imagined that he would do whatever he could to make her happy.

I rubbed my hand over my belly, thinking about our babies and how they might be coming into a world with a daddy who couldn't be there for them the way I wanted him to be. But how much could Dominic really handle? Between being there for the twins, as well as Olivia, there may not be much left for him to give to me if he's busy trying to make things work with Rebecca.

I'd been a single mom for so long that I knew I could handle it again. Mikey and Sally were older now, which meant they could help with the new babies. It wasn't the decision I wanted to make, but at the end of the day, I knew that we needed to walk away from Dominic and let him do what he needed to before he could walk away from us. I didn't want another repeat of what happened with Rick. I was older and smarter this time around, which meant that I needed to be strong enough to do what was right for everyone.

Thirty-Seven
Dominic

"Hey, Jane. Where are you? We need to talk," I called as I came inside and tossed my keys on the counter.

I knew that she was angry at me and didn't want to see me, but I also wasn't going to just walk away and let this go. I'd worked too hard trying to get Jane to let down her wall that I wasn't going to willingly let her slap it in my face again without fighting for us.

I walked down the hallway and found Jane sitting on the bed, rubbing lotion on her legs with a robe tied around her waist.

"Hey," I said softly, trying to keep my shoulders from reaching my ears with the amount of tension sitting on them. "Can we talk?"

She didn't look up at me as she kept rubbing the lotion in, which made me panic even more with how calm and aloof she was acting.

"There's nothing to talk about right now," she sighed heavily. "There's too much on my mind right now and between you and Rick, I can't take anything else today."

"What happened with Rick?" I asked, frowning deeply.

"He called to inform me that he's moving to Atlanta with his soon-to-be new wife, who is also pregnant."

I jerked my head, taken aback by the news.

"What? Just like that, he's up and moving?"

"Yup."

"So what does that mean for the kids?"

"Well, he wants to have them every summer."

"What did you say?"

"I told him no way in hell."

"Good for you," I said, finally relaxing enough to let out the breath that had been lodged in my chest. "I mean, the situation sucks, but good for you for standing up to him."

"Thank you. I haven't told the kids yet, but I'm sure they're going to have a hard time knowing that he's moving away."

"I can imagine. Is there anything that I can do to help? Do you want me to be here when you talk to them?" I didn't want to get my hopes up that there was still an *us*, but I was also relieved that she was actually talking to me and not shutting me out. This was progress, even if it was restricted to talking about her shitty ex.

"No," she shook her head, tears welling in her eyes. "Thank you, but no."

"Okay. Just let me know what I can do or what you need from me."

She covered her face with her hands and started crying. I rushed over and pulled her into my arms, trying to comfort her the best I could before she pushed me away.

"I can't do this," she sobbed.

"Do what?" I knew what, but I needed to hear her say it. If she was going to rip my heart to shreds, I deserved to hear the words come out of her lips.

"This—" she moved her hand between us. "I can't do whatever this is between us anymore, Dominic."

I stepped away, her words slicing right through me even though I expected them.

"What are you talking about? *This thing*? As in our relationship? As in, you agreeing to be my girlfriend and carrying *our* babies? That's not a *thing,* Jane."

"Please don't make this any harder than it needs to be," she begged. "I'm trying to do what's best for everyone."

"Who the hell said that you get to decide that? Why don't I have a say in it? Or Mikey and Sally? Why do you get to decide what's best?"

"Because I'm trying to protect them!"

"From what?" I yelled, my tone now matching hers.

"From having another man in their lives walk away, just like their father."

"Who said I was walking away? I'm literally standing right here, fighting for this to work, but you're the one pushing me away. I know that you're upset that I didn't tell you about Rebecca, but that's not a reason to just end this!"

"Because I have to! This is why I never wanted this to happen between us. I knew that in the end, I would be the one who would be left with a broken heart, picking up the pieces by myself. I knew better, yet I still let myself fall, and that's all on me. But I'm trying to stop this from getting any harder. Please, just let us be."

I shook my head and shoved a hand through my hair.

"I don't even know what to do with all of this," I stammered helplessly.

Jane wiped the tears from her face with the backs of her hands and let out a shaky breath.

"You still have a chance to do the right thing. To be the father that Olivia needs you to be. She has a chance to get to know her mom, you should let her."

"And what about the twins? Mikey and Sally? Am I supposed to just walk away from them? Because I can't fucking do that, Jane. And I can't believe that you would even ask me to. I'm not going to be the father that Olivia needs me to be and then be a shitty, absent one to the other kids."

"The twins aren't here yet, and when they get here, you can be as involved as you want. I won't keep you from them."

She didn't mention Mikey and Sally, but I could see it written on her face. I wasn't their dad, and she had no intention of ever letting me get close enough to try to be.

"This is insane; you do know that, right?"

Her shoulders fell as if she was giving up.

"I'm doing what's best for me and my kids, Dominic. I wish that you would respect that."

I pressed my lips into a thin line and thought about my words before I let them come out.

"And I really wish that you would get your head out of

your ass and see that I'm not Rick. You're punishing me for things *he* did, and that's not fair, Jane. You so desperately want me to walk away and give up on this, but you're the one who's given up. You're not even willing to fight for us. You're taking something that happened with Rebecca and blowing it up to be something more, just to have an excuse to end this."

She stood there quietly, not bothering to argue with me anymore.

"You know what, when you look back and wonder why this didn't work out between us—I hope you see that it was all on you. Because there hasn't been a single moment that I haven't been there and shown up for you and the kids. I love Mikey and Sally like they're my own, yet you fail to see that. You can't look past all of the times that Rick has fucked up because if you did, you would see that they have someone in their lives who wants to be there and who wants to be part of everything they do. Not just for the summer or when it's convenient."

"That's not fair."

"No, it's not. It's not fair that I opened my heart to you and you're willing to throw it away because you're scared. It's hard to trust sometimes; I get that. But you're not even trying."

"I can't! This thing between us should have never happened to begin with. Things were going just fine before I—"

"Before you what? Got pregnant? If that's the only thing you're focusing on in all of this, then maybe we were doomed from the start because I thought you meant it when you said you loved Olivia and me."

Her lip trembled as she tried to speak.

"I did."

My eyebrows rose to the top of my head.

"But you don't anymore?"

"I didn't say that," she whispered. "But this is all bigger than we ever talked about. We're not ready for all of this, Dominic. Don't you see that?"

I shook my head, pulled out a folded piece of paper from my back pocket, and handed it to her.

"What's this?" she asked.

"That's the house that I went to look at today before I got the call about Rebecca. I wanted to wait and take you and the kids to see it, but there were already a handful of offers, so I had to decide and move quickly. It has plenty of space for all of us—five bedrooms, an office, and a huge fenced-in backyard. It was perfect, so I made an offer on it because I wanted something that would work for *all* of us. I've never been in this for just me, Jane. I was ready for whatever came our way, no matter how big it was."

She covered her mouth and cried as I turned and walked out the door.

Thirty-Eight
Jane

"You're being stubborn, and you know it," Abby said as she slid a chocolate donut in front of me and sat down. "Just call him and tell him you were wrong about everything."

"But I wasn't. I meant what I said. Everyone will be better off this way, even if it sucks."

Abby shook her head and looked out the window of Rockin' Rooster while I sipped my vanilla latte. It was Saturday and the kids were with my parents again for another camping trip this weekend, giving me time to *pull my head out of my ass,* as my mom so eloquently put it. I wasn't sure who took the news of Dominic and me breaking up harder—me, the kids, or my parents. I didn't include Dominic in that equation because I hadn't talked to him since he walked out and left my house last week.

"How can you honestly say that?" Abby asked, narrowing her eyes at me.

"Because it's true."

"No, it isn't. Dominic isn't better off. The twins aren't better off. Mikey and Sally aren't better off. And you sure as hell aren't better off. I'm starting to think that maybe you don't know what the word *better* means."

"You're supposed to be supportive," I said, my frustration mounting.

"I am."

"By telling me how big of a mistake I'm making? Just because you don't agree with me doesn't mean I'm in the wrong. Trust me; I know what it's like to have someone walk away—I'm trying to protect the kids from having to go through that again."

"You're *assuming* that he was going to walk away, Jane. You didn't give him a chance to prove that he wouldn't. You didn't even talk to him about this, you just decided for him that your relationship was over."

"What was there to talk about? I don't want to go through this again, Abby," I sobbed, desperately trying to wipe the tears from my eyes before they could fall. "It hurts, okay? That's why I don't want to go through this again because I don't want to feel that pain again. Going through this with Rick was one of the hardest things that I've ever had to do because I saw how much it hurt the kids. But to have to go through that with Dominic—it will CRUSH me, Abby. It will destroy me in a way that I don't know if I'll ever come back from, and I'm not willing to go through that."

Abby sat quietly for a few moments while allowing me to gather myself. I wiped my eyes and then pushed the donut away, no longer wanting it.

"I know that you're hurting, Jane. I can see it. But you're letting fear hold you back from what you really want. You're using it to justify walking away because you don't want to risk getting hurt again."

"There comes a time when you have to cut your losses before it's too much."

"Yeah, and there's a time when you have to take chances because life is too short not to enjoy it. Jane, you found someone who loves you and your children unconditionally. Dominic has shown up for you time and time again. He's literally proving to you that he'll be there, but you keep pushing him away. You have to stop being so afraid of being loved and accept that you deserve it. Allow yourself to have that, Jane. I know that Rick did a lot of stuff to make you so distrustful, but Dominic isn't Rick."

I leaned forward and covered my face in my hands as I cried. Abby got up and wrapped her arms around me, holding me as I sobbed against her.

"I'm scared, Abby. What if he leaves?"

I pulled back and looked up at her with tears in my eyes. She gently wiped her thumb across my cheek, wiping them away.

"What if he doesn't?"

Thirty-Nine
Dominic

"What else do you need before I go?" I asked Rebecca as I set down the last bag of groceries we'd picked up.

"I think that's it. Thank you, Dominic. I appreciate your help."

"Not a problem. I'm going to head out, but if you need anything, call me."

"Will do."

I picked up Olivia and held her to my chest as Rebecca said goodbye to her. It was still a transition that was taking time for Olivia to warm up to her, but thankfully Rebecca didn't push hard or force her to do anything.

When I met up with Rebecca for a cup of coffee two weeks ago, I was surprised to find that she was clean and had the drug test results from her recent employer to prove it. While I didn't love that she had up and moved to Beaumont Creek without talking to me first, I couldn't shut her out of Olivia's life if she was willing to make an honest effort to be a part of it.

Apparently, the reason she'd been calling me before was to discuss moving here, so it was my fault for not giving her a chance to tell me. Over the past few weeks of Jane and I not speaking, a lot of things had gotten clearer in my head. Most importantly—not being an absent parent, which meant that I owed it to Olivia to have her mother in her life if she wanted to be. As long as she didn't hurt her, I was okay with letting Rebecca spend time with us. It would be a long time before I would feel comfortable allowing Rebecca to have Olivia by herself, but for now, we were taking baby steps and Olivia was getting to know her mom.

I buckled her up in her car seat and waved goodbye, feeling relieved that Rebecca had found an apartment to stay in instead of the motel. She had saved quite a bit of money before moving here and was able to put the deposit down, as well as had a few months' worth of rent payments set aside while she got on her feet with her new job.

I'd taken Rebecca shopping earlier to pick up some groceries as well as a few things she needed for the apartment. Thankfully, it was furnished, so she didn't need to spend any of her savings on furniture.

My stomach growled, reminding me that it was dinner time and that I had skipped lunch. I pulled into the parking lot of Surf 'N Shack, in the mood to overindulge in some fried food. I grabbed Olivia, and we headed inside. At first, I was going to get the food to go, but then I remembered how depressing the house felt lately without Jane and the kids, so I decided to sit down and enjoy dinner there instead.

I placed our order and then found a table in the corner of the restaurant. Olivia was situated in her highchair, looking at the book I kept in the diaper bag so she wouldn't be bored. A few minutes later, Capshaw headed our way with our drinks.

"Hey," he said, looking at the cups in his hand and then at us. "Is Jane not meeting you, or did we mess up the order?"

The pain in my stomach felt like he'd taken a knife and twisted it around my insides.

"No, it's just Olivia and me tonight." I took the plastic cups from him and sat them on the table.

"Oh, sounds good. Sorry, I'm so used to seeing you together that I thought the new kid messed up the order," he laughed.

I smiled, but it fell flat on my lips.

"Yeah, Jane and I aren't together anymore." I tossed the straw wrapper on the table and plunged the straw into my lid with a little too much force.

"Shit, I'm sorry, man. I had no idea."

"It's okay. We haven't really broadcasted it or anything," I laughed. "I guess I just assumed small-town gossip would do its job."

"Usually it does," he agreed. "I guess I'm just out of the loop these days. I'll go check on your food, but again, sorry about Jane. She's a hard one to get to commit."

I cocked my head to the side and studied him.

"What's that supposed to mean?"

"Nothing," he shrugged. "I just know that she hasn't had a serious relationship with anyone since she got divorced. She's dated a handful of guys since then, myself included, but no one can seem to crack through that stone wall she's built up. There was one guy—everyone called him the *Italian Stallion,* and we thought for sure he would be the one to break through since they dated the longest, but even he couldn't get past it."

I leaned back and twisted the straw, ignoring the obnoxious sound it made as it rubbed against the sides. Capshaw took my lack of response as his cue to check on our food and left.

I couldn't stop thinking about what he said and how no one could seem to get past the impenetrable wall she'd built around herself. I knew that she was guarded because of Rick, but I hadn't realized just how shut off she really was. Early on, she'd pushed me away whenever I tried to get closer to her, but I just assumed it was because she was nervous about how the kids would take it. But now I realized that wasn't it at all. It was because Jane was too scared to allow anyone to get close, and once I did—she shut down.

I might not have gotten over the wall, but deep down inside, I knew that I had started to chip away at it, and that's what freaked Jane out the most.

Forty

Jane

"Doctor Nicoli will be in in a few minutes," the nurse said as I climbed up onto the exam table for my ultrasound. She left the room and closed the door behind her.

It felt weird not having Dominic here for it, but I also hadn't reminded him of the appointment either. Four weeks had passed since we'd last spoken, and even though he was giving me what I asked for—I still hated it.

I'd spent the past few weeks thinking about what Abby had said, knowing she was right. But that didn't mean I was going to run back to him and beg him to take me back. Maybe it was the universe working things out for us and I didn't need to get in the way. Deep down, I still worried that he would walk out and leave us, just like Rick did. That was a feeling I couldn't shake, no matter how hard I tried. It was also the one thing that fueled me to keep moving forward, accepting that Dominic was no longer going to be part of my future.

There was a knock on the door, so I put on my best fake smile and waited for Doctor Nicoli. The door pushed open, and my eyes widened when I saw Dominic walk in instead.

"Hey," he said casually as if he was supposed to be there and didn't somehow just turn my world upside down by showing up.

"Hi. What are you doing here?"

"I'm here for the ultrasound. I wanted to see the babies and make sure everything was okay."

"Okay." I dug my fingers into the paper beneath me and tried not to fall apart in front of him.

He sat down in the chair beside me and rested his ankle over his knee. He was so calm and cool that it made me even more anxious. But he was here for the babies, and that was all. I couldn't be upset about that, especially when I'd promised him that he could be as involved in their lives as he wanted to be. Even if we'd gone weeks without talking to each other. It wasn't about me right now—it was about the babies.

Doctor Nicoli came in shortly after and began the ultrasound. If he'd heard the rumors around town about Dominic and me splitting up, he didn't say anything. He went on with the ultrasound as if everything was fine, so I focused on doing the same.

"Both babies are doing well," he said, moving the wand across my stomach. "Were you guys interested in knowing the genders?"

I chewed my lip nervously, too afraid to look at Dominic. This wasn't something we had talked about, and now didn't feel like the time to try.

"Whatever Jane wants is fine with me," Dominic said.

Doctor Nicoli nodded and then looked at me, waiting for my answer.

Deep down, I wanted to know what we were having so I could start shopping and prepare the nursery that was currently being set up in my now cramped bedroom. But I didn't want to spoil the surprise for Dominic if he didn't want to know yet.

"Umm," I said, stalling for time while I tried to decide.

Dominic shifted next to me, and suddenly, I felt his hand on mine. I gasped quietly at the contact, hating the way my body betrayed me when I laced my fingers through his.

"We'd like to know," Dominic answered, looking at me instead of Doctor Nicoli.

"I don't want to ruin the surprise if you want to wait," I rushed out before anything was said.

"I'm okay with knowing. I can tell that you want to, so I'm on board with it too."

"You don't have to—"

"Jane," he said, my name a warning on his lips. "Trust me; I'm fine with this."

"Okay." I released my bottom lip that I had been holding between my teeth and nodded at Doctor Nicoli, who was patiently waiting for us to decide.

"Wonderful," he replied warmly with a smile. "If you look closely, you can see that Baby A is a boy." He pointed to the spot on the screen that confirmed this. "And Baby B is a girl."

I watched his finger move across the screen and point to the other baby.

"Thank you," I whispered, still feeling the heat from Dominic's body as our fingers stayed intertwined.

He continued the rest of the ultrasound, collecting the measurements he needed and logging the information into the computer. Once he was done, he grabbed some tissues and wiped the goo off my stomach before printing a few ultrasound images for us.

Dominic lingered around and waited for me to schedule my next ultrasound before walking me to my car. I had expected him to say goodbye and jump into his truck, but instead, he stood beside me with his hands shoved into his pockets, looking ridiculously sexy.

"Thanks for being there today," I said, feeling the heat pulse across my cheeks, suddenly feeling embarrassed about being glad he was there when I'd worked so hard to push him away.

"Thank you for *letting* me be there today," he replied with a wink.

I tried to smile, but it turned lopsided, and I felt like I might look like I was having a seizure, so I grabbed the car door and opened it.

His hand reached out and grabbed it, stopping me from getting in as his arm blocked me.

"Can we talk? Please?"

I stood there paralyzed, afraid to move because my body might touch his and if it did—there would be no turning back.

"I know you're scared and want to run," he said softly, tucking a strand of hair behind my ear. "But you don't have to, Jane. You don't have to push me away and do this by yourself. I'm not going to hurt you, but I understand that you're guarded and need to take your time with this. I'm also not going to walk away easily. I refuse to leave without fighting for what I want, and Jane—I want you. I want these babies. I want a life with you with *all* of our kids. A big house that fits all of us comfortably. A family, Jane. That's what I want, and I'm not backing down until I get it. So if you're determined to keep fighting me on it, we're going to have to figure out how much fight you have left in you because I'm not backing down."

His hand dropped from the car door and rubbed my belly. My eyes closed, and I prayed that the tears burning beneath the lids would go away.

"I love you more than anyone I've ever loved before, Jane. And I will spend the rest of my life proving that to you. Making you feel worthy of my love because you are. You deserve so much, and I'm going to give it to you every chance I get. But you've got to stop fighting this, Jane. Stop fighting me."

My breath hitched in my throat as I tried to swallow down the emotion that was bubbling up inside.

"I'm scared," I admitted with a whisper.

"I know you are, baby. But you don't have to be."

"I don't know how to do this, Dominic. I'm going to mess it up. At some point or another, you're going to get tired of it and walk away. It's inevitable."

"No, it's not. You just have to step back and let me in. This doesn't have to be hard or scary, Jane. It's okay to allow yourself to rely on me; I promise I won't let you down. Neither of us is perfect, and we're both going to make mistakes—but if we work as a team, we can be unstoppable. I don't have the secrets to making a relationship work, Jane, and I can't tell you that this won't have its ups and downs, but I know that we owe it to ourselves to at least try."

I lifted my hands to my face and covered it as I cried. Dominic turned me, so I was pressed against his chest as he held me and rubbed my back.

"But what if this doesn't work out? I asked softly.

"The more important question is, what if it does?"

I laughed and shook my head.

"How can you be so confident? Aren't you even a little afraid that this could all go sideways?"

"Of course I am," he replied. "But I don't want to focus on what can go wrong when I can stand here and look at all of the things that are going right. If you focus your energy on the negative and everything that can go wrong, that's what you're going to get. But if you redirect that and look at all of the beautiful and wonderful things happening to you, those things will grow and multiply."

"Just like these babies," I joked.

"What can I say? I have super sperm."

He gave me a wink with one of those panty-melting dimpled grins, and I knew I couldn't fight it any longer. He was right—I could sit around and wait for bad things to happen because I expected them to, or I could look at all of the good things and work to make more of them happen.

"So, what do you say, Jane? Can we give this another try?" he asked, wrapping his arms around my waist as I linked mine behind his neck.

"Yes," I replied with a grin that split my cheeks. "But we have to go slow—baby steps. I'm an old dog, and it's going to take some time to learn new tricks. I can't just shut off the worries and doubts that linger in my head, but I'll try to work on it. I've been doing this on my own for so long that it's going to be an adjustment for me to let you in and help out, so please be patient with me."

His smile was enough to brighten the sky around us, lifting the rest of the dark haze that had been lingering around me for weeks.

"Are you okay with all of that?" I asked.

"I'm sorry, all I heard was dog and then I started picturing taking you doggy style, and that's all I got from it."

I pursed my lips together and swatted his arm.

"You're so bad! I'm being serious, Dominic," I scolded playfully.

"I know, I know." He grabbed my hand before I could hit him again and brought it to his lips. "I heard every single word you said, and I'm on board with all of it, Jane. You're not doing this on your own anymore. We're a team and I've got you."

"Thank you."

"Alright, now that that's settled, let's get you home so I can do you doggy style."

He spun me around and pushed me toward the car eagerly.

"Dominic!" I laughed loudly, loving how light everything felt now.

"It's been four weeks of not being inside of you, Jane, and I'm not waiting any longer. You head to your house and grab some food on the way. I know you get hangry, and I don't want that getting in the way of all of the makeup sex we have in store for us. Also—call your parents and see if they can take the kids for the next three or four days."

"Three or four *days*?"

"Yeah, what I have planned for you is going to need your undivided attention and lots of naked sexy time."

He slapped my butt as I climbed into my car and buckled the seatbelt.

"See you soon," he promised before rushing off to get into his truck.

Epilogue
Dominic
2 Months Later

"Fuuuckkk, baby." My eyes rolled back in my head as Jane's lips tightened around my cock. "That feels so good."

She moaned against me, the gentle vibrations traveling straight up my shaft and to my balls that she was massaging with her free hand while the other stroked me.

"I'm getting close, baby," I warned.

Her lips parted as she flattened her tongue, taking me deeper into the back of her throat. Then she closed them tightly, hollowing her cheeks as she sucked mercilessly until my fingers were tangled in her hair and ropes of cum were eagerly swallowed. Once I was done, she pulled away, kissing the tip of my cock as it hung limp with satisfaction.

"That was incredible," I said, helping her to her feet. "Though we were supposed to be picking paint colors."

"What can I say? That tan color reminded me of your cock and I wanted it." Jane shrugged and wiped the corner of her mouth.

"Well, I would love to repay the favor; however, Nate and Abby will be here soon with the kids so we don't have time. But, tonight, I plan to devour that pussy and make you come so many times you don't even know what day it is."

"I'm six months pregnant with twins and constantly exhausted," she joked. "I don't know what day it is most days to begin with."

"Well, at least tonight you'll have orgasms to blame for it."

We walked through the house, looking at the other paint samples we'd brought for the nursery. Shortly after we decided to give our relationship another try, we started house shopping together as a family. After several open houses and browsing online, we finally found our forever home.

It was a beautiful, two-story house with vaulted ceilings and an open floor plan that joined the kitchen to the oversized living room that was plenty big for our expanding family. We also loved that it was a six bedroom, three bathroom house with an additional family room upstairs that we could use for the kids as they got older and wanted their privacy.

The kids had already picked their bedrooms and were out picking up their chosen paint colors for the rooms while Jane and I decided on what color to paint our bedroom and the nursery. Our parents were headed over shortly to help with the rest of the painting while Jane and Abby were assigned to rest in the living room that had already been painted and aired out so they could stay clear of the fumes.

"I think we should go with a gray in here," Jane said, walking around our master bedroom. "Maybe some accent colors to brighten it up, like yellow or orange. Maybe even a pop of pink?"

"Whatever you want, baby," I said as I wrapped myself around her from behind and rubbed her stomach. My phone vibrated in my pocket, which just so happened to be resting against her ass.

"Is your phone ringing, or are you just happy to see me?" she joked.

"Both." I laughed and pulled it from my pocket to see a new text message in our group thread.

Nate: We're grabbing food. What do you guys want?

Abby: We're stopping at Surf 'N Shack, do you guys want your usual?

Nate: Let them pick, Abby. They don't have to eat there if they don't want to.

Abby: WHO doesn't want to eat there? It's delicious.

Nate: I don't know, people who like to eat something other than fried fish and hush puppies for every single meal?

Abby: Don't start with me. I'll sit on you and smother the life out of you.

Me: Ummm. Surf 'N Shack is fine with us.

Nate: You don't have to give in to peer pressure, bro.

Me: I don't want anyone to be smothered…

I laughed as Jane pulled her phone out and started reading the texts.

"I wouldn't mind if you smothered me," I whispered, letting my hand roam up over her breast. "You could smother me all day, every day."

"You're so nasty," she teased. "But I like it. Almost as much as I love hushpuppies."

Jane: Can you get me my usual but add an extra side of hushpuppies? Please and thank you!

Abby: Yesss! I want an extra side too.

Nate: Capshaw said there's a hushpuppy shortage.

Abby: Stop. Lying.

Nate: It's true. Apparently they can't keep up with the demand around town lately. I guess two pregnant women have been taking them all.

Jane: Better yet, change my fries to all hushpuppies.

Abby: Oooohhh (drooling emoji)

Jane: No, I want the fries too. Ugh, this is so hard!

Me: I'll do my usual, but please substitute my fries for hushpuppies.

Nate: Not you too! Come on, man!

Me: Happy wife, happy life.

Nate: You're not even married and you're already whipped.

Me: No, but maybe someday soon. I'm paving the way to her saying yes with hushpuppies. Better yet, order all of the hushpuppies they have. Just add it to my tab.

Abby: Yay!! You're going to make the best brother-in-law ever!

Nate: Or until he runs out of hushpuppies.

Abby: Why don't you HUSH your mouth and let me have my moment?

Nate: I'll give you a moment if you want it. (winking emoji)

Jane: (eyeroll emoji)

Jane: We have to get back to work but thank you for grabbing food. I'll give you some money when you get

here. Please, please, please do not forget the hushpuppies.

Abby: We got it. You can treat next time.

Nate: We'll be there soon. Just look for the van that shows up filled with stupid hushpuppies.

Jane: That would literally be the best day ever.

I tucked my phone back into my pocket and kissed the side of her neck.

"You know, maybe I'll save a hushpuppy or two for later tonight," I growled lowly in her ear.

"Oh yeah, and what are you going to do with them?"

"That's for me to know and you to find out."

I tickled her sides, making her laugh. I never thought I would have the perfect life, but this was proof that I had all I could ever want, along with two sweet babies that I couldn't wait to meet.

****

**Want to see how Jane and Dominic are doing with the twins? Be sure to grab their bonus epilogue here:
https://BookHip.com/NTLHCGL**

Ready for more? Find out if Capshaw has finally found his happily ever after in Third Time's The Charm here:
https://books2read.com/u/b5lEyG

Looking for something more thrilling to read? Be sure to check out my small town romantic suspense series! Start 'Til Death Do Us Part here:

https://books2read.com/u/m2RJNR

Other Books By Samantha Baca

The Haven Brook Series
(small-town romantic suspense):

'Til Death Do Us Part (Haven Brook Book 1)

https://books2read.com/u/m2RJNR

The Cradle Will Fall (Haven Brook Book 2)

https://books2read.com/u/b6O0QE

The Ties That Bind (Haven Brook Book 3)

https://books2read.com/u/mqgoz8

A Very Haven Christmas (Haven Brook Book 4- Novella)

https://books2read.com/u/mvqGjj

Three Strikes, You're Gone (Haven Brook Book 5)

https://books2read.com/u/mvqL2z

<u>The Dark Shadows Trilogy (romantic suspense)</u>

Five Steps Ahead (Dark Shadows Book 1)

https://books2read.com/u/38Q0gO

Ten Seconds Too Late (Dark Shadows Book 2)

https://books2read.com/u/3JRgVB

Against The Clock (Dark Shadows Book 3)

https://books2read.com/u/m2YwoR

<u>The Stone Creek Series (small-town- novellas)</u>

Chocolate Covered Mistletoe (Stone Creek Book 1)

https://books2read.com/u/3LRk9N

Candy Coated Promises (Stone Creek Book 2)

https://books2read.com/u/mldP5Y

Pumpkin Spiced Possibilities (Stone Creek Book 3)

https://books2read.com/u/bojdwV

<u>Beaumont Creek Series (small town)</u>

Just One Time (Beaumont Creek Book 1)

https://books2read.com/u/3G52zK

Second Chances (Beaumont Creek Book 2)

https://books2read.com/u/4Aj6Z0

Third Time's The Charm (Beaumont Creek Book 3)

https://books2read.com/u/b5lEyG

Four-ever Single (Beaumont Creek Book 4)

Preorder link coming soon

Fifth Wheel (Beaumont Creek Book 5)

Preorder link coming soon

<u>Whiskey Mountain Series (small-town-novellas)</u>

Something To Talk About

https://books2read.com/u/4X62ag

Something To Think About

https://books2read.com/u/3GWAan

Something To Believe In

https://books2read.com/u/3yVzgB

Something To Live For

Preorder link coming soon

<u>Sugarplum Falls Series (Holiday Novellas- can be read as standalone)</u>

Blame It On The Mistletoe

https://books2read.com/u/bw1rqe

Blame It On The Eggnog

https://books2read.com/u/38PPY6

<u>Standalone Books</u>

One Last Wish

https://books2read.com/u/mqg7D9

Finding Love In Apartment 2C (novella)

https://books2read.com/u/bze9aZ

Cocky Counsel: A Hero Club Novel

https://books2read.com/u/31Kzkn

All Is Fair In Food And War (novella)

https://books2read.com/u/bp8qjX

<u>Holiday Books (novellas)</u>

Snow Place To Go

https://books2read.com/u/4A560N

A Christmas Wish

https://books2read.com/u/4EKXpE

Holiday Hijinks

https://books2read.com/u/4DP6Ze

Acknowledgments

Thank you so much for reading Jane and Dominic's story! I hope you enjoyed it as much as I loved bringing their story to life! If you happen to feel so inclined to leave your thoughts in a review, I would greatly appreciate it!

To my alpha and beta readers, thank you for your constant support and for helping me through another one! You all bend over backward to make time to read for me and I love that I can message you with random ideas and you'll help me sort through them. You're the real MVPs!

Tillie, thank you for taking on another book for me! Your editing skills are so valuable to me and I love reading the side notes with your reactions as you move through the story.

I wouldn't be able to do half of what I do if it weren't for my family and their ongoing support. I'm a lucky girl to have such an amazing team of cheerleaders and to be so loved!

Richard, you are the light of my life. The happiness on my darkest days. The keeper of my secrets—shhhh, you swore you wouldn't tell. The proofreader of my words. Designer of my covers. Formatter of my books. And master of my universe. A little over the top this time with my acknowledgment?? No way! I love you and appreciate everything you do for me.

To my girls—you're getting older and more curious about the stuff that mommy writes. Trust me when I say there will be a time when you're older that you will *wish* you didn't know what I write… Until then, thanks for being my best supporters and being so excited when you see my books. I love you both more than you could ever know.

To my ARC team—thank you for signing up for another book! I hope you've enjoyed it and I look forward to the other books I have coming your way this year!

Thank you to everyone who has taken the time to read this book as well as the acknowledgements. If you're looking for more words from me, don't forget to check out my backlist!

About the Author

Samantha lives in the southwest with her husband and two small children after abandoning her childhood dream of living in a cabin in Colorado when she found that she couldn't afford to live there and was deathly allergic to the woods. When she's not writing, she's usually spouting off sarcastic remarks while drinking wine out of a coffee mug to look like a functional adult while chasing down her toddlers. She enjoys spending time with her family, watching reruns of Friends, and the 24/7 flow of coffee that can be found in her veins. Be sure to follow her on social media for updates on what she's working on.

You can find her here:

Facebook: https://www.facebook.com/AuthorSamanthaBaca

Instagram: https://instagram.com/author_samantha_baca

Goodreads: http://www.goodreads.com/authorsamanthabaca

Facebook Reader Group:

https://www.facebook.com/groups/2945710968775398/

Webpage: https://authorsamanthabaca.wordpress.com

Newsletter: http://eepurl.com/g0NcSj

www.ingramcontent.com/pod-product-compliance
Lightning Source LLC
Chambersburg PA
CBHW022023310726
48972CB00006B/1781